WHOSE COFFEE IS IT?

WHOSE COFFEE IS IT?

JUNE AKERS SEESE

ARPress
45 Dan Road Suite 5
Canton MA 02021

Hotline: 1(888) 821-0229
Fax: 1(508) 545-7580

Ordering Information:
Quantity sales. Special discounts are available on quantity purchases by corporations, associations, and others. For details, contact the publisher at the address above.

Printed in the United States of America.

ISBN-13:   Softcover   979-8-89389-009-9
              eBook   979-8-89389-010-5

Library of Congress Control Number: 2024907091

Table of Contents

Dedication ix

Acknowledgements..xi

Chapter 1 1

Chapter 2 7

Chapter 3 11

Chapter 4 15

Chapter 5 17

Chapter 6 19

Chapter 7 21

Chapter 8 27

Chapter 9 29

Chapter 10 33

Chapter 11 35

Chapter 12 37

Chapter 13 39

Chapter 14 41

Chapter 15 45

Chapter 16 47

Chapter 17 49

Chapter 18 51

Chapter 19 55

Chapter 20 57

Chapter 21 59

Chapter 22 63

Chapter 23 67

Chapter 24 71

Chapter 25 75

Chapter 26 77

Chapter 27 79

Chapter 28 81

Chapter 29 87

Chapter 30 89

Chapter 31 91

Chapter 32 93

Chapter 33 97

Biography...99

CRITICAL PRAISE FOR EARLIER WORK

What Waiting Really Means

This witty little book skitters nervously from topic to topic, recording Mary's clever apercus, chronicling her odd habits, and cataloguing her obsessive dreams…a brittle first novel that amuses with every crack.

—Kirkus Reviews

Is This What Other Women Feel Too?

Seese's voice is tough, lyrical, and darkly funny… her writing is fragmented but engaging, and the cleverness of it is that you can't always tell the wisdom from the wisecracks.

—Detroit Free Press

James Mason and the Walk-In Closet

There is a kind of bad news that goes far beyond the serial killings or the neglected children or the brush fires or the black ice that we read about every day. June Akers Seese is the mistress of what is probably a universal female sorrow. The women in these 13 stories have been alienated from conventional roles, but remain unliberated by the feminist movement, and are thereby stranded in silent anguish between 2 worlds, belonging to neither. The woman in the title novella states: "I don't pretend to understand my life. I sleep with a defrocked priest and work for a man who likes boys. There's then and now. Then I lived in Scottsville. Now I live in Dublin. Then I had a job and the Irishman and what passed for an ordinary life. Now I have what's left."

—Washington Post Book World

Some Things Are Better Left to Saxophones

"*Some Things Are Better Left to Saxophones* is terrific, both in the colloquial sense and the root meaning of the word."

—Stephen Brill, Professor of English Literature
and Film Studies at Wayne State University.

A Nurse Can Go Anywhere and Collected Short Stories

June loves stories—and not just the kind you find in books, but stories you dream up of overheard conversations, family secrets, whatever was left unsaid the last time you hung up the phone. She collects them, hoards them, and then transforms them into fiction. Her immediate gifts, then, are a sharp eye and quick ear—making her a kind of spy, voyeur, but also a guardian angel. She sees but she also sees through. She's vigilant but she's also tender.

Writing about the blood and mystery under life's surfaces puts her in the current of some of the best writing being done today. This is fiction that's lean, somewhat tight-lipped, un-flashy, and careful. It's built on suggestion, not statement. And it pays no more attention to plot than ordinary life seems to do.

June's writing is of this strain, but there's a difference—a difference built up from her deeper gift. That gift is empathy. June's writing rises in power because she's down in the skin along with her characters. Mining the covenants and conspiracies of ordinary life, she's not at all detached. She's a participant. Someone who's been there—and hence understands.

—Paul Evans, Editor, Southline Press

Dedication

For Sandra Commito who realizes a friendship with two viewpoints is twice as strong.

Acknowledgements

I would like to thank Shula Lazarus for laughing at my best lines and for realizing what lies beneath them. I would be remiss if I did not include my gratitude to the entire Hebebrand family and especially Karl Hebebrand whose idealism and endurance continue to sustain me. My thanks also go to my sons, Robert and Matthew Seese, whose photographs cover my office walls and make insomnia easier to bear. And, finally, to Alan Sorensen who knows all about endings and is not afraid to speak his mind.

Chapter One of *Whose Coffee Is It?* appeared in
*Many Mountains Moving: A Literary Journal of Diverse
Contemporary Voices*
Vol. X, No. 1, 2010. It was nominated for a Pushcart Prize
on December 2, 2010.

Chapter 1

They don't see me coming. I'm a surprise. Not invisible. Bypassed. But not in this shop drinking coffee from my monogrammed mug. There are hundreds of us. Customers. And, unlike me, most of them are not here every morning. Being overlooked is new to me. Until I was 70 it didn't happen; but now, eight years later, I know I have to get used to it. The inevitable must be faced or things get worse. A woman my age with bleached hair and thick make-up is grotesque —besides, I'm too tired for masks.

The coffee shop is full of smells from Santa Domingo to the House Blend. The air conditioning works. Music plays. Everything but heavy metal and rap, so I don't get blasted off my stool. The clerks are all in college or law school and they like their work. They will even split the O.J. and pour half in a thick glass with ice.

I pay attention to details, and I listen to strangers: the arrangement of their words, their pauses, evasions and little movements. It's an international place. Spanish is in the air, but French, too, once in a while. Sometimes I learn more than I want to know from a man in love with his cell phone. Truth is slippery. I can only speculate, but I have time to do just that.

What is acceptable here? What passes for normal? I'm not sure, but some people get too near the edge and have actually been barred. One man was cruel to the clerks; he called it "teasing" and he tried to get a political rise out of the regulars, but he was met with silence at every turn. After four months, he just stopped coming. He drove a fancy car and liked to gloat over the erosion of Democratic power after 9/ll. Maybe his wife got sick or he moved to Florida. Age brings change, sooner or later. Life brought it later to me. My husband and my best friend died in the same month. It's been a year, and the weather hasn't changed. It just rains more this summer, and sometimes the power fails in the late afternoon. Atlanta is a city of trees. Some fall.

This whole neighborhood hates change, not just the old folks. Protest groups have formed to fight legal battles and to pester the zoning board about a new house that looks like a poor man's castle with a false fourth floor and a three car garage. Concrete monuments to bad taste have replaced ordinary colonials and split-levels. It has become a community of tear-downs. Trees mean nothing to these builders; down they come too, and a new house goes up. Sod is laid and a few shrubs added. It's hard to tell who the owners are; they don't have children who play on the front lawn or hang out the windows.

In July, the power didn't go out, but the heat increased, so I only traveled from the swimming pool in my apartment complex back to my bedroom where the grab bars above my tub make me feel safe. Sunbathing in a wide brim hat with bottled water and sunscreen at the ready seemed a thing of the past. For a few weeks, I took a nap before and after lunch. I fell asleep in my recliner digesting a few pages of *Reading Lolita in Tehran*. Then after my tuna sandwich, I crawled between the sheets with the curtains drawn, my bedroom dark and cool. Sometimes I even used a light quilt. I don't pay the electric bill here.

The dog days of summer. Only nobody has one. A tenant smuggled in a kitten and got caught. She didn't last long. There's a waiting list, so they can enforce the rules. 98 degrees, 95 degrees, 97 degrees. One day follows another and the sidewalks steam up after the rain when it does come. Then I go out again and sit by the pool after dark, and think about my husband. He liked air conditioning on low, worried about the light bill, bought store brands, and cringed at the idea of a T-bone steak until the day he died. We didn't have to worry about money then. I used to listen to his stories about sharing an unfinished basement with an aunt and her wild son. Only a curtain separated the two families. He and his sister ate kidney beans out of a can and too many pancake suppers; a far cry from the fresh squeezed orange juice and granola that he came to expect from me every morning.

Sometimes the best way to be heard is to whisper; but I couldn't whisper. Recovering from laryngitis, I stayed in my new apartment at first. I moved in on Memorial Day weekend, and if I took the holidays seriously, I'd have the blues as well as a halo of silence. So I played it safe and sat in front of CNN with a tall glass of lemonade. Veterans passed before my eyes: World War I, World War II, the Korean Conflict, Operation Desert Storm, and now the war in Iraq, yet to be given a title. What I didn't see were the coffins covered with stars and stripes or the newest veterans with missing legs; young men who believed they were invulnerable. Men who might have survived motorcycle races or an impulsive dive from a cliff, had they not enlisted.

Once I moved beyond the confines of my apartment and the pool, it took me a long time to settle into the rhythms of the coffee shop. It wasn't just the laryngitis I had that first month. Or age. There were other older women who came in; but none who stayed long. The first man I got to know is the one I like best, a Special Ed teacher who graduated from law school but couldn't pass the bar. I like modesty and I don't pry, so I didn't ask how many times he tried.

John/John, the famous two year-old who saluted his father's coffin and who ended up somewhere in the Atlantic Ocean separated from his bones, tried three times before he passed. I once had a black friend who got in on the quota system back in the fifties, and I never asked him either; but he didn't give up, and finally set up practice in his father's law office. We've lost touch. So you can see how little I know about law school and the bar. I don't even watch *Law and Order.* My husband did, but he's gone and I try not to think about him all the time. It's hard not to.

The coffee shop brings relief. Everything distracts. The regulars come and go. They move away or get too sick to make the effort. Some die. Last week I went to a wake and it is all we talked about the next day; but nobody said a word about the corpse looking natural. I imagine there are customers who think twice before spending all that money for a Grandé Latté when Folgers Instant waits at home, but coffee has little to do with it. One man, a few years shy of retirement said, "All they need is a shower here and I'd have everything I want!" He's getting a divorce and sometimes his wife comes in with him. One morning a carefully turned-out honey blonde in beige and chocolate brown came through the door. "That's our divorce attorney," he said. "She's retired and only works part-time. Nothing's cheap!"

Anyway, my friend who couldn't pass the bar comes every day too, but never at the same time; so we cross paths only three or four times a week. His name is Saul Bachner, and he's from New Jersey. His father was a cabbie, so he has a repertoire of stories that has yet to run dry. All about stickball and kids he went to grade school with, about last minute tickets for Broadway musicals and the price of property on the Jersey shore. He's kept up with his friends and made new ones. It's easy to see why.

My friend is not a showboat, and his sense of humor cracks me up. He's retired too, from the DeKalb County School System. Tall with a head full of white hair, he must have been an imposing figure behind a lectern. Now he's careful with his money and though he's always going off on a cheap flight to Costa Rica or Prague, he buys his clothes at Value City and drives a car that's seen better days, carefully. There are no dents in it. He often walks to the coffee shop. It's not far. He owns an apartment building *up the road apiece,* as they say here in the New South. He lives in one of the apartments and keeps an eye on things. Something is always breaking down, and he usually knows how to repair it. Eric Hoffer once said, "Maintenance is everything." And the longer I think about that quote, the more it covers.

Before my husband died, we had a tree-trim party every Christmas. Everyone brought an ornament or a bottle; and some brought both. Bachner brought a huge pecan pie from Costco. He knows a bargain. People fought over it and they thought I made it myself because I slipped it onto a crystal plate before the guests started arriving. For my birthday, he gave me a little eyeglasses holder, a pottery thing for my bedside table, so my glasses wouldn't fall on the floor. Bachner knows all about old age too.

Today, there were bombs in London. Some exploded underground. One blew the top off a bus. Time passed and there were more bombs. The bombs were impotent, but the police shot a man who wore a heavy overcoat. It was hot in London and the man ran from the police. Who knows why? He was an electrician going to work. There were apologies and explanations and the days dragged on. This week a new version of the story emerged, but one thing was sure—there were seven bullet holes in the electrician's body.

More than one customer at the coffee shop said, in so many words, "We're next! The Center for Disease Control already has those big rocks between it and the sidewalk." Soon an argument started. "Big rocks? Don't you mean boulders?" Would it be New York, DC or us? They might speculate all day. I ordered a Russian tea biscuit and a refill.

Soon, iced coffee replaced the usual, and the regulars switched from pottery cups with their initials inked on the sides to tall plastic glasses. A few diehards drank espresso. Headlines continued to focus on gas prices and the war. Atlanta's homeless are now forbidden to beg from tourists, and today, Coretta Scott King had a stroke.

One customer moved to Florence but came back to close on her former house: "I'm writing a pamphlet on how to survive the boat over," she said. She is a widow too, almost 50. Radiant. Florence has a lot in common with Paris (all that art and literary history) and I've never been to either place so I'm jealous. But that doesn't stop me from reading coffee table books in color at the library. I can barely pick one up; they are so heavy with culture.

Everything is new here: the coffee shop, the whole shopping center, and my apartment complex. But it wasn't always that way. It's hard to find words for what was replaced. For years, a motel stood in back of the former strip mall. Men and women rented rooms by the hour, and business was brisk. It took me awhile to catch on. Three afternoons in a row, a tall woman in stilettos with two-inch platforms and a silver mini skirt, sauntered by with her companions—a different one each day, all bald, wearing suits and conventional ties. No money was exchanged in public, but I overheard plans for a tryst as I walked by on my way to Baskin Robbins. By then a police precinct had moved in, and the liquor store did more business than the grocery. I stopped buying ice cream after dark and eventually the store moved out, along with a branch of Kinko's and a Laundromat. So imagine my surprise last winter to return from a trip to the East Coast and find two bulldozers and a rock pile where that strip mall had been!

A group of hard hats stood surveying the mall ruins. They had already begun work on the new apartment complex too. I'm not an optimistic woman, but these images changed me, at least for a while. I was the fourth tenant to sign a lease, and even then there were plans to expand the apartments up a hill, in back, where the motel used to be. I like it here on level ground. The first floor seems a wise choice for the future.

Chapter 2

Advice I got from accountants and *Good Housekeeping* gurus about preparing for widowhood shouldn't have been overlooked, but I overlooked it. For years, I drove around town with five dollars and one credit card in my wallet. I even charged groceries. Of course, Wes paid the card off every month, and it provided an instant record of my expenses; but the real reason for the card was kept between the two of us. I couldn't balance a checkbook.

Once a bank manager told Wes, "Bring your wife in and I'll be glad to teach her the basics in two hours." I ignored his offer until Wes died. Then I was up to my ears in paper: trusts, insurance policies, the will, income taxes, inheritance taxes, estate taxes. Would a financial advisor know much more than how to keep his percentage of my profits? I doubt it. For awhile, I dated a CPA who rescued me from all that paper. We had little else in common, so gradually I stopped watching Turner Classic movies with him at my side on Friday nights. I can be bored alone.

I pulled back and took a good look at myself. What could I expect at this late hour? Uncertainty was at the top of my list. I was in good health except for a T.I.A. that made driving risky. "Strokes happen in a series, if you're not lucky," my neurologist told me. I have never felt lucky, so I made some changes.

The first thing I did was collect on the life insurance. Our house and cars were automatically paid off, so I sold them. Why not? MARTA stops at the end of my street, and cabs are everywhere. I had plenty of patience and a smart realtor. Next, I found a painter for the inside of the house, the trim around the bricks, and I bought a potted plant for each side of the front door. It wasn't hard. A yard sale, a neighbor's truck to haul the leftovers to Goodwill, and then off to the movie matinee so the house was empty to show. Within three weeks I signed a contract. The cars took a little longer, but we didn't lack for high school boys on our street who considered them a *steal.*

I didn't go far, and I knew what to expect because I had been watching the strip mall for over a year. It was two miles from my street, and a world away as well. Now, I walk from my new apartment to the coffee shop each morning. I never lose my way; and when I get there, I feel full of the familiar. When I consider the fact that only two years ago these rooms were not here, and that any minute now I might not be here, this predictability means all the more. Even the sidewalk and the parking lot that connects the two places seem safe from bulldozers and bombs.

So I leave every morning with high expectations. When I walk out my apartment door, I know I'll soon be in the thick of city life, that the heat will be transformed into cool air that I can breathe. Some days I stay close to the counter and other days I take a table by the window. The dark in the back of the coffee shop where the couches wait is usually not where you'll find me.

I thought I'd get accustomed to the steady decrease in power that age brings; and perhaps I will eventually. For now, I try to keep my balance. I have a sheet of daily exercises, easy ones, that help me steer clear of the walls and not keel over; but there are no such gimmicks to make me satisfied with what's left of my editing career. I had taught a writing class at Callanwolde Fine Arts Center on Tuesday evenings for ten years, and now I edit the work of a former student who is looking for a publisher. I have spent far too much time going over this student's manuscript. I have to restrain myself. It is not my memoir. I offer suggestions, sometimes cut whole pages, and certainly tinker with paragraphs; but it is his life and he gets to decide how far he wants to go into the past. He has already written 300 pages. He is a brave man, and his is a story of a fall from power too. Red barns and acres and acres of rich Ohio farm land left behind and finally replaced by a shack in the Deep South; years of fried mush for breakfast and greens with only the faintest taste of grease for dinner. His entire family separated from things of this world—trying to make sense of an afterlife.

My student dismisses his mother's looks; only her actions—going door to door with religious pamphlets in the cruelly hot North Carolina summers—and her weary trek home. I am free to imagine her, and the image in my mind comes from that famous photo left over from the Great Depression of a thin, sorrowful mother in a James Agee photograph. My student does what he's told. He creates a world and pulls the reader into it—a forlorn world. It's no wonder he has writer's block from time to time. We meet at the coffee shop once a week to explain my cuts and examine his occasional perfect sentence.

I don't lack for entertainment. Cable TV and Net Flicks have made movie theaters irrelevant. It's a good thing because driving is too risky for me. Last night "20/20" had a story that stopped my heart. The topic was shocking, but the real horror was revealed as an Amish girl walked along a country road. She had been raped; first by an older brother, then by a younger brother, when the first boy left home. In the barn while her parents were in church. When, at last, she found the courage to tell a state trouper, her mother, while awaiting the trial, took the girl to an Amish dentist who pulled all her teeth.

The girl was 16, and as she spit blood into a bucket, she looked up at her mother:

"Why?" she managed.

"Guess you won't be talking much now!"

Her brothers were given six months of being shunned by the Amish community, and the girl was mercifully taken out of her home and sent to foster care in another city. By the time she graduated from high school, someone had bought her false teeth. In the Amish community, most girls only attend school through the eighth grade.

After that show, I didn't fall asleep until 4 A.M. Even John Cheever's stories of New York "when men still wore hats and a Benny Goodman Quartet could be heard outside a cigar store door" couldn't remove the imagery of that godforsaken Amish barn and unpainted frame house from my consciousness. I am opposed to home schooling. If parents are crazy or if they offer only neglect, their home schooled offspring don't have a chance. Home schooling is popular though, and often the scores of college freshman who were home schooled are higher than scores of public school graduates. But home schooling can be an easy out for those whose hatred hides behind the words they use. Sometimes there are leaks:

"Hell will freeze over before my daughter goes to school with Mexicans."

"I know what you mean. It took me weeks of drill to make my grandson stop saying 'axed.' *Those people* will never speak the King's English."

Chapter 3

The minute I walked through the door of the new apartment model here at Northwood, I felt relief. Grays and beiges, tans and creams smoothed out the living room's angles and settled into the hardwood floors. There I stood with the rental agent who had enough good sense not to confuse me with facts and figures. I had the brochure in my hand and I asked him a few questions while I leaned against the stove and marveled at the layout: a walk-in closet the size of a tiny room plus a single bedroom just big enough. The best part: I was in charge of what came here with me, and I could unpack when I was good and ready. Freedom is a heady thing, but Janis Joplin was wrong. She told Bobbie McGhee a big fat lie on that train. It's not, "nothing left to lose." The words sounded right then, but she was too young to know the whole truth. I'm not sure I know it.

So the outside world rolled on while my world diminished. A few days ago it was confirmed that Coretta Scott King had had a massive stroke. Today she said a few words, and her doctor added a few more in front of a microphone outside Piedmont Hospital. The woman protesting the war in Crawford, Texas, said more than a few words until her own mother had a stroke in California. Now an ad saturates the TV channels with the ghost-like image of a silent, rigid woman who waited too long to go to the ER when her symptoms struck. It's a long ad on how to prevent a stroke; and it gives me the creeps because I still remember the details of being rushed to the hospital and the 4-hour wait for a room. I had no notion that anything was wrong with me. I was eating breakfast at R.Thomas with some friends. How could I have known that my eyelid suddenly drooped, or that my conversation was not up to its usual level? Had I been alone, I might be as bad off as Mrs. King—struggling to speak with my right side paralyzed. Unable to walk.

I continue thinking of Mrs. King and her lifelong familiarity with bomb threats as I walk to the coffee shop and back home afterwards; but while I'm there, the other customers distract me. Today the owner's four kids paid a surprise visit along with their grandmother. They were showing off their new school supplies and ordering O.J. for their thermos bottles—their tiny hands pressed against the display case. Just watching them cheers me up. I don't want to let go.

School starts earlier every year. The traffic has returned to the surface streets, and last minute shoppers pop in for a quick iced coffee. A TV announcer says that beaches are forsaken, what with hurricane threats and rushed-up school openings. But I'm a long way from the beach in Atlanta, so sand and sharks needn't worry me. The war drags on, yet the imagery of Abu Ghraib torture does not recede with time. Talk today at the coffee shop centers around inadequate body armor and stepped up recruiting in inner city parking lots. Nobody mentions a draft. The clerks have seen the Michael Moore movie. They won't talk about it; but I can't help thinking of dusty camouflage uniforms and work boots. The owner's offspring are laughing now, a reminder that cherished children still exist.

Two men are pointing their fingers at each other in an argument about Supreme Court decisions. Where is justice to be found? They agree that revenge seems easier to locate. What would William Faulkner say from his grave in Mississippi and would he add anything to his famous question: When will I be blown up? I don't know, but I continue reading and looking for answers and I keep these thoughts to myself. But I'm not reading Faulkner today; I'm pushing through V.S. Naipaul's essays on Muslim countries, written 20 years ago, after his visits to Iran, Malaysia, Pakistan and Indonesia. I'm also rereading a yellowed copy of *Persian Nights* by Diane Johnson. The novel scared me the first time around. Women were not safe in Iran then, and nobody seems safe now. Today the temperature has soared to 100 degrees and the owner's children are climbing into their mother's new SUV.

August 20th is my wedding anniversary. I think backwards to our first celebration when we ate the top layer of our frozen wedding cake in my mother's backyard in Hartford, then to one or two romantic celebrations at a four star restaurant in New London and then to an inn overlooking the Connecticut Turnpike. There are big gaps in my recollections after we moved to Atlanta 30 years ago. We spent a few anniversaries at *Eat Your Vegetables* before it left Little Five Points, and we had one blow-out at the Ritz. Until it closed, my husband bought me earrings from Geode at Lenox Square. Opals, gold twists—all one of a kind—but the years passed and an opal fell off its backing and I lost one twist. Still and all, our marriage did not break apart.

We traveled together: conferences every year, a trip or two to London, up and down the New England Coast to visit friends, back and forth to DC, and to Old Saybrook where my older sister settled before we lost track of each other. My husband and I never lost our love of New York or New Orleans in the spring; but I don't dwell on these getaways. And I certainly don't dwell on my sister: "You should have married a real doctor," she told me more than once.

Not a morning passes at the coffee shop without travel talk. Last year it was Croatia. This summer, Amsterdam. Whether it's a week with frequent flyer miles or a layover on the way to Greece, getting away seems to be part of the answer for everybody but me.

"I have a direct flight on KLM, eight hours," Bachner speaks first.

"Great. It's an international city. More than a red district," a man fresh from Bolivia offers.

"You mean red light district?"

"Yea, Amsterdam has everything: trolleys, bridges, a train station built like a castle, cobblestone streets."

"They have cobblestones in New Jersey. And a zoo," Bachner likes to argue.

"Why would I want to visit a zoo? I grew up near the Bronx zoo. I've seen the Pandas at the zoo in D.C. more than once. What do I want with animals in this heat?"

"It will be cool in Amsterdam in September. You'll need a sweater, maybe a trench coat."

"I should take spending money," Bachner continues.

"Don't look at me," a single woman chimed in.

"How is the Euro?" Bachner asks the most important questions last.

"A few pennies more," answers a self-appointed expert who reads *The Wall Street Journal* every day.

Everyone went back to their newspapers. All this travel talk doesn't faze me. I'm staying right here and glad of it. I can't walk to the branch library in this heat, and the woman who sometimes gives me a lift is one of the travelers, so I've looked over my own shelves and decided to reread John Cheever.

I've stacked a supply of Cheever on my nightstand: his letters, journals, and interviews, even a bio, plus a paperback of his short stories with a missing red cover and some loose pages. It's not the first time I've reread those stories! I've never been able to finish Cheever's novels, except for *Falconer*. I have a passion for prison literature but no deep interest in New England towns like St. Bolophs. In fact, I once put together a course in prison literature at Callanwolde that featured work by Truman Capoté, Norman Mailer, and Mailer's protégé, Jack Abbott; the notorious killer who shot a Puerto Rican waiter because the waiter didn't serve up Abbott's Sunday night supper to his liking. Shot him dead on the sidewalk outside a Manhattan restaurant. Mailer took flack for that error in judgment for years.

Imagine, Mailer getting Abbott a publisher, a room in a boarding house, being the voice for a second chance at a parole hearing, and then *The Belly of the Beast* turned out to be Abbott himself who emerged from all those literary cocktail parties to promote his memoir, only to land in the slammer once more—leaving blood on the street and a gun not far away. But I'm digressing. The subject is prisons, and John Cheever's voice is the one I crave.

Cheever lived in Ossining, New York, home of Sing Sing prison where he taught writing before and after the Attica riots. So, for now, I'm all tied up in Cheever, expecting this heat to subside. And by the way, no one signed up for my course but an ex-convict. After all, in 2005 crime is up close and personal, and the public only wants to read about it in formula mystery novels, not literary fiction! That's what Saul Bacher thinks, anyway. "Better stick to the memoir," Bachner reminds me that it's still popular in spite of James Frey's lies.

Chapter 4

Gas prices get higher every week (Six dollars a gallon rumored at one station in Dunwoody), but the news no longer bothers me. Without a car, I am free of insurance and repairs too. Yet this sudden rise in price is big news at the coffee shop. "Three dollars a gallon across the street," a landscape architect rolls his eyes. Bachner takes out a calculator. This week, talk about the war in Iraq has reached a peak. The mother in Texas and the anti-war celebrities who followed her were on *The Today Show* this morning. The regulars at the coffee shop remember the Vietnam War and Lyndon Johnson's fall from grace, but they don't say much about it. Someone always changes the subject before sides are chosen, and the waitress is more diplomatic than a foreign ambassador.

I save my attention for the six o'clock news. Peter Jennings died last week. He's been off the air since April, so I have moved over to CNN. Sometimes I resort to keeping it on for hours with the sound muted. The silence is soothing and I can still read the scroll on the bottom of the screen whenever the fancy strikes me. I need TV to fall asleep. I worry about my health more than I ever have. I dream about IV's and blood pressure cuffs. I ruminate on the pleasure of a morphine drip.

In the spring, I went in for my annual check-up at the gynecologist. The nurse, a woman not more than ten years younger than I, moved a step behind her perky mask into what was certainly a canned speech for senior citizens. "Do you keep busy?" she began in a voice so patronizing I wanted to tell her I was a professor, still lecturing; but that would have been a lie. I just smiled and pulled the paper sheet closer to my neck. "You'll need to remove those pretty sandals before you get your legs in the stirrups. I just love to see the elderly dress in bright colors! So cheerful, and that's important. You need to keep your spirits up! You're awfully quiet today. Is something bothering you?" She held my chart close to her chest. I kept smiling and that unnerved her, so she returned to what should have been her questions in the first place. "What medicines are you on? What dosage? Do you remember?" Then she stuck a thermometer in my mouth. At last the doctor walked in with a commentary on my memoir class. His next door neighbor has taken it twice. At least the doctor sees me as a person. He even warms his instruments. It was the nurse's turn to shut her mouth.

Today, the sounds of the outside and the music inside mingle, making such a mess in my head that I can't concentrate on the news or the pain in my mouth. It is two hours until my appointment with the oral surgeon. I have those giant x-rays in a manila folder, a bottle of pain pills not worth the powder to blow them to hell, and a sealed letter from my internist, Jerard Cranman. I've seen him for thirty years and he knows as much about medicine as American Literature, which is a lot. If I had my way, all my doctors would be English majors.

Chapter 5

Once last week, I walked out to the pool with a beach towel under one arm plus my apartment key on a chain around my neck. The sun wasn't in sight, and not one single person was near the pool. The man with the net who removes bugs and brown leaves was probably still sleeping. As soon as the water was up to my shoulders, I did a few stretches and surveyed the scene. The lounge chairs were all even and there wasn't a weed in sight. The flower beds here are small. I could weed them myself if I took a notion; but the lawn service yanks them up before they offend anybody. I looked at the remaining blooms with dew weighing them down. The sun had come up by the time I finished my stretches. A dead bug floated near my hand. I stood still and watched it pass. Its wings were longer than its body—an iridescent shade, almost green. Not a roach or a ladybug; I couldn't be sure what it was.

So I continued my routine and swam around the sides of the pool, then the short distance from one side to another. It's not shaped for laps. I splashed around for awhile before the sounds of the morning intruded. Just as I was about to leave, the bug floated by again and I was surprised by its front legs; thin as a piece of thread. They were moving. The bug was alive. A car engine started up. A door slammed. Ladybugs bore me, but this creature was captivating. I continued watching as I wrapped my beach towel around my body.

The day passed. Nothing else happened, so I took a long nap and then turned on the TV. As I lay in bed listening to a weatherman worried over New Orleans being below sea level with only a few August days left and about to meet Hurricane Katrina, I thought of that bug —its wings heavy with water, unable to fly away or escape, being carried along by the waves, and about to be removed by the pool cleaner. Then I thought of the roach that I stomped after wiping bits of cheddar off my kitchen counter. I know that roaches wait for darkness and dripping faucets before they run over the floors and scurry up the cabinets searching for warmth and rest in the metal plates surrounding the burners on the gas stove. If I spray, that's where I find them in the morning.

The apartment complex has a generator, so our lights may fail, but not for long. This storm is supposed to bring its edges to Atlanta; fierce winds and thunderstorms, but nobody is leaving town because of it. I should feel safe too. After all, I'm prepared: candles, a case of Ramen Noodles, a radio with batteries. But it is three o'clock in the morning and I'm wide awake, watching the scroll at the bottom of the TV screen again. The Louisiana Governor has called for a mandatory evacuation of New Orleans, my husband's favorite city. We have been there for conferences a dozen times and I intend to go back next year and stay in the French Quarter one more time. I'll never forget those getaways.

Somewhere on my book shelves are journals I wrote on little spiral tablets as I waited for Wes in the New Orleans heat. We took siestas every day. Other times, I sat in courtyard cafés drinking mint tea, reading *The Times Picayune* and debating the extravagance of buying a custom made hat for $200. I never bought one, but each visit gave me the opportunity to exercise my imagination in two hat shops across the street from one another. We were even there for the World's Fair, a failure to be sure, but we had wonderful nights at a little residential hotel on the trolley line. It had an outdoor café too, right on the sidewalk. I still have a postcard with a picture of *A Streetcar Named Desire* filed away somewhere. And a postcard of the trolley too!

Chapter 6

The afternoon crowd at the coffee shop is younger and different. It's Labor Day, and I've moved to a couch by the windows. *The New York Times* lies on an oval coffee table at my feet. A man is reading the personals in *Creative Loafing* across from me. We are separated by the coffee table, a narrow thing topped by a collage of city scenes. I can see the bare shoulders of the women in the ads. The man wears a wedding band and a Rolex. He sips espresso from a dainty cup.

It's another scorcher. Outside the window sweat collects on the forehead of a man wearing black jeans and a Forsyth County tee shirt. His eyelid is pierced along with the little space below his lower lip. I can't see his tongue, but I wouldn't be surprised if metal had invaded his mouth as well. A tattoo runs the full length of his arm and a steel chain falls all the way to the sidewalk from a loop in his belt. He is biting his fingernails and smoking a cigarette at the same time—one hand for each! Whatever he's saying doesn't travel through the window pane.

I can't ignore the exchange at a table behind me. New Orleans is on everybody's mind. Animal rescue teams have been getting a lot of play today. The folks who are left in the city don't want to leave their dogs behind; and one man has nine. "I got an easy solution for those dogs and it's cheap," this from a soft voiced man beside me. "A 22 bullet costs about a penny and one thin dime will do the trick!" The woman next to him says nothing. She's a regular in the mornings and has left her Labrador Retriever tied to a post outside. She tears up and refuses a refill. The man who was hoping for relief in the personals finally walks out with his cell phone, and sits at a table on the deck near the dog.

On television and everywhere I look things are falling apart; and I have to pull myself up from my chair to go to the bathroom, so absorbed am I in this anarchy. Outside, the temperature has fallen to a perfect part of the eighties—Indian summer as they called it in Connecticut. The leaves here are still on the trees, but the air is what I remember breathing in with pleasure and hope in those long ago days. September should be a month of beginnings. School starts. Styles shift. Summer reruns are mercifully over. But this fall, school started in mid August and the Gulf Coast winds tried to carry destruction to a place never before seen in America.

Houses in New Orleans now look like something out of *The Three Little Pigs*. Piles of sticks. Dead bodies float in streets. Men in uniforms are everywhere: the army, the national guard, policemen from near and far, wildlife rescue; and celebrities like Sean Penn wax eloquent on the power of individual effort. He's not the only famous person to appear and get his hands dirty; but the other celebrities blur in my mind because the faces of the dehydrated children and terrified women press close. Then a street musician has words for the host on NPR: "I lost my house, and I can't find my uncle." A pause follows a little static, and I hear the solitary sound of his trumpet. The musician is famous too; and he came by bus to Baton Rouge; but "only for a little while," he says. I mute the T.V. and turn off the radio.

Chapter 7

I still remember the coffee houses of the fifties: in Manhattan, Greenwich Village, and San Francisco. I wore black ballet slippers then until the leather cracked. Kerouac and Ginsberg were never my favorite writers, but they were upfront in those early days and the smoky places where they hung out drew me in. They called it a beat generation, but I never really felt part of it. Didn't I work overtime? I didn't start out as a wife or a mistress though living together on the sly had some glamour then. A sense of mystery and romance went along with it. But I waited and watched for a long time before I took that risk.

I met Wes at a gallery opening in West Hartford. He was wandering through the framed photographs, and he looked every inch an insurance executive. Hartford is the home of the insurance business, and gray flannel was the uniform in those days. Wes had gone to summer camp with my date, an actor who eventually dropped out of Yale Drama School, but that, as they say, is another story. That night, the three of us came back to my apartment where we continued drinking and talking about the theatre. Lloyd Richards was getting his start at Yale then, and my date was a name dropper; so Wes and I listened to him brag about his time in New Haven. He told us how innovative the Long Wharf Theatre was; how Hartford Stage was conventional by comparison. My windows were open and sirens on their way to the city hospital were hard to ignore. The wine soon ran low and the only thing left in the refrigerator was a bottle of Channel No. 5; so I went to the pantry and returned with some stale Saltines. Neither man showed any signs of leaving.

My date progressed to the history of the Cherry Lane Theatre in the Village; more inside information. One thing for sure, Wes was a good listener. "And what do you do?" I proceeded with a question any book on manners would have forbidden. But I was a little loose by then, and bored with my date who had rolled this monologue my way once before.

"Well, I spend a lot of time in the library when I'm not looking for a job." Wes was going to make me dig for an answer. "Wes is a microbiologist." My date knew one thing I was not interested in was DNA. The evening dragged on. We ran out of Saltines too, and when the two men left together, I put on a Chet Baker record and looked out the window. Nobody walked by, and the sirens were quiet long enough for me to fall asleep on the day bed. Fully dressed.

It may seem like an odd path from microbiology to psychiatry, but it happened gradually, and the logic of it made sense to me. Wes' Master's was in Medical Microbiology and he fully intended to go on for a Ph.D., but the summer in question left him alone in the lab because his major professor had left for a Fulbright in Cairo. Wes kept a pot of coffee on a Bunsen burner all day, and smoked too many cigarettes in the cafeteria. Then one of his buddies from high school, a first year medical student, came down with lung cancer and was dead by Christmas. Wes wasn't the only one who quit smoking and ended up with a bad case of nerves.

Wes took a step back, still not knowing exactly what he wanted to do, and applied to medical school; thinking if he continued to be soured on research, he would at least have some choices. If he changed his mind about the lonely lab, an M.D. might put him at an advantage. Forget about our courtship; it was fun and it lasted a long time. By the time Wes graduated from medical school, he still hadn't made up his mind about a career. It was during his internship that the choice became clear. By then, he was certain that the lab was not for him; and suddenly two options came his way.

First, the head of Orthopedic Surgery tried to talk him into that specialty because Wes has always been good with his hands. Carpentry. Pottery. I still have the little clay figures his mother proudly showed me. About that time, Wes came home with an invitation for the two of us. We were living together by then, and money was tight, when a nurse on nights, the widow of a popular psychiatrist, offered Wes her husband's personal library. She had already donated his textbooks to the medical library at the hospital.

"We could be bringing home *Reader's Digest Condensed Books* for all I know," Wes told me on the way to the nurse's house. By then, he had learned a few facts about her husband. Dr. *Lawler* hadn't been out of his residency but five years and he was dedicated; saw patients at his house as late as 9 p.m. and all day Saturday. He had his first heart attack a year ago; cut back his hours, stopped smoking, lost twenty pounds, and took a vacation. He still did a lot of pro bono work, but he did it before 6 p.m. Yet he died four months later of a second attack.

When we got there, the doctor's books had already been boxed; and his wife offered us a beer. Wes was on call, but I took one. We made small talk and left. All the way back to our apartment, we listened to the car radio. I don't remember what was playing, but I know we kept our thoughts to ourselves. When we lugged the boxes up the stairs to the third floor and opened them, I was thrilled.

Novels, biographies, collections of essays all related to psychiatry; and Lawler was inscribed on the title pages. He didn't use his first name. Weird, I thought. But that entire year, Dr. Lawler provided our social life. We read his books and took long walks to talk about them. We had missed the movie *David and Lisa*, but got to read the script. All of the books: *Pathways to Madness*, a Jules Henry collection of essays; *A Definitive Bio of Freud* in three volumes; Eric Fromm, Karl Menninger, all the first-hand accounts of survivors of state mental hospitals; *The Snake Pit* by Mary Jane Ward, plus that famous handbook by Freda Fromm-Reichmann, *The Art of Psychoanalysis*.

Dr. Lawler's books filled six shelves. I suppose my favorite was *I Never Promised You a Rose Garden* by Hannah Green, later Joanne Greenberg. It was a thinly disguised autobiography of a schizophrenic girl who was treated by Dr. Blau (Freda Fromm-Reichmann) at Chestnut Lodge. I forget what they called the hospital in the novel. Recovering from a psychosis in the fifties included the possibility of cold packs and shock; right before the *zines* revolutionized state hospitals. It's a lyric novel, a work of art. Joanne Greenberg went on to become a well-respected minor novelist, but I didn't follow her work. In the early years of the paperback revolution there was so much good stuff to read that I couldn't go on with what seemed to me lukewarm fiction.

Wes came home one day to tell me: "They once asked Dr. Reichmann whether she would use drugs or intensive long term psychotherapy to treat schizophrenics, if she could only choose one approach. 'Drugs,' she replied. A significant statement when one considers that she spent her life and all her clinical research treating inpatients with psychotherapy, mostly schizophrenic inpatients!"

My idea of bliss became listening to Wes and reading Lawler's books. I was not interested in microbiology or orthopedic surgery, but psychiatry was another story. In fact, it was me who pushed Wes away from those little saws and all that mucking around with paste and plaster. "You would be forsaking a life of the mind. All you would become is a good technician." Yet another reason Wes chose psychiatry was his allergy to rubber gloves, for it soon became clear that he had one.

"Go see one of the attending physicians before you make up your mind," his mentor told him as he was about to pick a residency. He did, and when he saw the surgeon's hands, he applied to the Institute of Living. It was right in town, and one of the four finest private psychiatric hospitals in the country. We had walked outside the brick wall that sheltered its beautiful grounds many times. Courtesy of Dr. Lawler, we now owned a stack of those green and white psych journals, so even I knew of Francis Braceland, the grand old man of American psychiatry, (if one forgets the Menninger brothers in Kansas momentarily), who had been the Director of the Institute.

We got falling down drunk on a bottle of champagne the night Wes opened his letter of acceptance. Our future hung there, in that moment, the spilled champagne blurring the logo on the stationery. So began the hardest three years of my life. Sure I had a job, a profession; but it was in many ways as if I too was feeling the anguish of Wes's patients in those three years. Proofreading seemed like child's play, by comparison. As solitary as it was precise.

Wes was part of a small first year residency from all over the world: a French Jew who had been a messenger boy during the Holocaust and his psychologist wife who was teaching their two boys French and swimming—their oldest child was four. A tall doctor from South Africa who met his wife in Dublin where he interned—he was an Indian exiled from India, and under South Africa's apartheid he was classified as an *other*, so his wife could never go home with him. A local Italian fellow; plus a bona fide Italian from Italy.

The two of them joked about being put aside in a profession founded by Freud and heavily populated with Jews. "Wait till Silvano Arieti comes," the local Italian said. In the spring, the Institute would be 100 years old and we couldn't help but be awed by all the upcoming lectures and parties. "Silvano Arieti is the one who did all the work on the schizophrenogenic mother, and then confessed in public that he was wrong." We all admired his honesty and his courage. So Arieti came in the spring and opened his lecture with: "I come from five generations of Italian Jews..." We couldn't afford his book on psychiatry and creativity. I bought it years later when I began teaching "The Memoir: Reading and Writing It."

There were a few light moments like these, but comic relief was in short supply that year. Four residents fell by the wayside; one had some sort of collapse, one was asked to leave because he thought he already knew everything, and one quit the first week and is now a pediatrician in Albany. His assigned patient was tearing up a unit and the resident was two days late reporting for work because someone had stolen his car and his clothes in Manhattan—too much stress for anyone! Wes' best friend was a seven foot tall ex-coroner from New Orleans, a former star on the LSU basketball team, who had aspirations to be an administrator. I learned that fact ten years later on our first visit to New Orleans. "Imagine that. Your best friend was famous *and* modest – a winning combination," I mused. "You are right, Darling; psychiatry is never boring." I crawled into bed and found my place in his arms.

Chapter 8

So you can see what a bright new world psychiatry seemed at first. A life of the mind filled with men and women who wanted to relieve suffering and who believed they could. Men who questioned, argued and laughed. Men who seemed whole. There were actually three women in the residency program, and they fraternized with the wives. One was a former nun and the other two women had gone to medical school at Columbia. Both were members of a book club for the staff and residents, so we joined the club only to discover that a woman had never before been a presenter. So the nun became the first and I followed her. We were considered trail blazers. Sometimes I counted the days until these monthly meetings.

All during the master's program in microbiology, (and bear in mind, it took two years), no professor had given a party. Microbiology has its share of loners. Wes had two close friends in the program, so we traded off evenings with hamburgers and six packs; and played boring games of Scrabble. The six of us popped a few corks on New Year's Eve, but nobody had enough money to throw a real party. Then, during the last six months of the program, when it was near time for evaluations, one wife, whom I took an immediate dislike to, sent out insipid little invitations for a Saturday night buffet. I called to tell her that we were coming, and spent the next two weeks wondering what the evening would be like.

There's a certain amount of shop-talk at any party; but this affair was in a class by itself. It was immediately obvious that the hostess was trying to advance her husband's career, and she had gone to a lot of trouble to do it. No pot luck. She had prepared gourmet dishes, and spaghetti was not among them; neither was the tuna casserole so popular then. She even baked the bread.

There was the usual milling around at first. I tried to balance a plate, a drink, and a flyaway napkin; and since I know nothing about biology, cheated my way through chemistry for a D, and had no interest in listening to men who talked in monotones about the frontiers of research, I smiled a lot and listened to the other wives trade stories about breast feeding and "rooming in." Next, we proceeded to refill our glasses and find a seat. The guest of honor sat in an easy chair, I had a footstool, and Wes sat on the floor.

The hostess milled around, fawned over the professor and pretended to be interested in his story about breeding a pinto mouse. The tale stretched on for the better part of an hour; and one would think the pinto mouse carried a plague threatening the city to see the wide-eyed attention paid the professor. It took all the restraint I had not to laugh out loud.

I knew Wes inoculated rats in the lab. Cats too, maybe, but I tried not to think about the needles and cages. I'm not an animal lover, but the imagery bothered me. I wanted to fade into the wallpaper at this party. Instead, I tried thinking about what we would do in bed when we got home, but I couldn't concentrate on those details either. Was this to be our social life in the years to come?

I behaved myself, didn't take a third drink, and didn't lock myself in the bathroom with *Time Magazine*. I watched the others. They spent a lot of time eating. We weren't the first to leave, and that took a bit of doing. On the way home, all I said was, "What is the point of a party if you can't relax?" Wes was quiet. "Even surgeons pontificating on tying knots would be more fun than this!" I knew, even then, when to stop talking!

Chapter 9

Oscar Wilde was right about drink being the curse of the working class. A little further up the scale, martinis are their own special curse. Memory being what it is, the lemon twists or olives begin to blur, hospital conversations pick up and finally fall with a lot of overlaps in between. One final dinner party in Connecticut outshone all the others. After it was over, I never went to another hospital function or invited more than three psychiatrists at one time to our own celebrations. Things descend into shop talk fast: administrators who don't give a rip about patients, insurance companies that dictate medical care; and all true but none of it interesting to anyone not working in the field.

I once thought that Lawler's library would be my basis for informed questions and fascinating arguments, but I was dead wrong. One night in the hospital cafeteria I ate supper with Wes and a third year resident. I guess I wanted to show off, if the truth be known, so I initiated a discussion about that 3-volume set of Bowlby's research on child development. "Who's Bowlby?" the resident asked. I was speechless. The latest volume had been touted at length in the previous Sunday's *New York Times Book Review;* and I thought that fact alone would be enough to make the book a hot topic. Well, maybe, if Dr. Lawler could have risen from his grave with a cigarette in hand. Safe now underground, at least *he* would want to hear about Bowlby. I thought a lot about Lawler that fall. In some ways, he was a bridge to Wes and our new life at The Institute. I had time to think about a lot of things. Wes was on call more than he'd expected. He slept in a little house on the grounds in a huge bed that had been special ordered so the 7-foot resident wouldn't have his feet dangling over the end.

Yet I wasn't lonely. Wes called home in between emergencies. "I wish you were here with me," he whispered.

"I wish I were too. Maybe we could share your scrubs," I whispered back. Eventually, I made friends with one of the wives, the only one, who, like me, had no children. Sometimes, though, I complained to her.

"You expect too much", she said, "Our husbands don't have time to sleep, let alone read Emily Dickinson to us. The Institute of Living is not an eighteenth century salon."

She was a Comparative Literature major from Columbia and I satisfied myself with listening to her stories of Lionel Trilling back when he was the star of the English Department and the words *New York intellectual* still meant something. One real friend can pull you through, and she was it. But I am straying from martinis and psychiatrists; those take-it-off-the-income-tax hospital parties where nobody really wants to be there, where anyone at the dinner table with sense and a rich fantasy life keeps their mouth shut and leaves early. This approach worked until one Saturday night when I drank like the others and watched things fall apart.

It started with slurred words I couldn't comprehend. Then the doctor to my left stood up just as the soup bowls were cleared, "You have insulted my wife, sir," he proclaimed to the man on my right. Silence followed and I never did figure out the nature of the insult. Later his wife said, "Pay no attention to all John's teasing. Our boy acts like a girl, and we have done everything—bought him cowboy outfits, baseball mitts; nothing helps." Her husband then dropped his head in the mashed potatoes, and soon after left the table for the bathroom where I later threw up on the hostesses' quilt—a handmade treasure from her grandmother. Someone had draped it over the towel rack. I felt so bad; the next morning I sent a dozen roses to the host with a letter of apology. I had left one suede shoe there too; and it came back on Monday night with a note pinned to it: "How can a nice Jewish boy marry someone like you?" And Wes wasn't even Jewish. It must have been his horned rimmed glasses and beard. A stereotype to be sure! I don't remember saying anything beyond, "I've had enough paella!" In fact, I have no memory of what they served for dessert.

"You let a few things slip," Wes told me. The hostess' husband was insufferable —if we need a clinical category. In the end, nobody would work with him, but his reputation didn't stop me from thinking: Why *did* Wes marry me? I knew the answer, and it wasn't for my sterling self control.

Wes married me for my mind, or so he said; certainly not for my winning ways under the sheets. Though who knows how all of it comes together? I learned about sex from *Webster's Unabridged* and the *Reader's Digest*; and I tried hard to be a good girl. None of this book-learning helped much, so I was very, very careful. Ignorance and fear go together. The summer I graduated from high school, wedding plans for others seemed to pop up out of the blue, unbidden; and they scared me. I had a boyfriend but we didn't go far enough for him, so we broke up the week before the Senior Prom.

That June, my best friend fainted after teaching a Sunday school class in the Methodist Church we both attended. By the time she began rushing to the bathroom before we walked to work, I had guessed her secret. We hand dipped ice cream at a café a block from the high school for $1 an hour. My mother must have known the truth all along because she pulled back and didn't force scrambled eggs on either of us. We wore white uniforms and tennis shoes to match, and we were careful not to miss a night of removing their scuff marks. My friend didn't miss a day of work until October when I was away at college with a new life of mixers, smokers and bonfires for Homecoming weekend. Her wedding announcement was my first piece of mail at the dorm. A birth announcement soon followed. I held tight to a scholarship to Bowling Green University in Ohio, not far from Toledo where we drove on blind dates for 3.2 beer and about as romantic as a Wednesday night prayer meeting, which, by the way, I had attended that last summer, so bored was I with Manchester, Connecticut. I was a bridesmaid in two weddings that Christmas, and they were rush jobs too, so the following summer was full of baby showers I didn't attend.

I spent my sophomore year in the college library looking for the meaning of life, having left John Wesley and his orderly principles behind in a history class. Then I hung around with gay men as soon as I learned what one was. They were safe. Getting pregnant might ruin my life, and any girl with brains in those days knew rubbers broke—not that I ever saw one. I kept up my grades, kept my scholarship, and worried about the future. While other girls in the dorm played bridge and knitted argyle socks after supper, I sat on my top bunk, content to watch them and copy my class notes on 3" by 5" cards. The most exciting thing that happened that year was a bus trip to the Toledo Museum where the drawings and oils by Van Gogh were displayed. It was my first visit to an art museum; and I was drawn to *The Potato Eaters*, a vision of gloom and poverty that seemed more real than his *Sunflowers* or *Starry Nights*. The following summer I worked at an upscale furniture store in Hartford and learned a lot about Knoll and Eames. I had a close call with a furniture salesman, and then I met Wes.

Westcott Arwood. It was his voice that brought me to his side. He could make a sentence sound like a lyric poem; add that to a sure sense of touch, and I was his. I knew how important it was to love your work—to have a choice in what you did all day. I intended to continue to work hard, and so did he. We believed in work, in the future. The last thing we considered was immediate gratification. The price was too high. So we became engaged without a ring. I went back to Ohio in September, and Wes answered my letters with a barrage of post cards. I still have them in two shoeboxes in my walk-in closet.

It is important to sleep with someone you can talk to about all the things that matter; and in those early days everything mattered to me. The only thing that didn't matter was what I'd yet to experience. Wes and I talked on park benches, on blankets in the shade of trees I didn't care to know the names of, and in cafeterias in the hours before closing. We talked until the chairs were cleaned and stacked on top of tables; until the catsup bottles were taken from the booths and a dishrag passed over the slick surface between us. With or without a sandwich, it all seemed like a picnic to me. My mind skips to the nights after work years later when I would hold Wes's head in my lap on the couch. This was our ritual for a long time, even when he was too tired to talk. When we moved to our final house, I wanted to buy two recliners so that we could rest, side by side, and enjoy a mutual sense of collapse; but I didn't. Time passed, his hair went from salt and pepper gray to white; and then his hairline receded. He was bald when he died.

Chapter 10

Today, I wandered around my apartment waiting for the *New York Times* to hit the door. When it didn't, I looked for it every ten minutes to no avail. So bound by routine am I, my whole morning seemed destined to fall like dominoes leaning in order. I boiled my usual egg, watched the sand fall in a little timer and ran more cold water over the egg than necessary. Soon I was lost in another *dream*.

Wes and I had boiled eggs in a Pyrex coffee pot that sat on a hot plate in our first apartment. I have always been an early riser, so I would wait, half-asleep, in a kitchen chair and watch the bubbles rising from the eggs while Wes slept. The days were long then, and we both worked too hard; but my happiness lay in the softness of those mornings and the memory of what had just happened in bed. It is always summer in this memory; though the eggs boiled year round through winters that held plenty of gray slush and waiting at bus stops. Where the wind forced itself into my coat and made me wish for all those clothes that L.L. Bean offers in their catalogue—clothes destined to last forever. Clothes I couldn't afford. I was taught never to buy name brands then; but I got over it when Wes entered private practice.

This morning I ate my egg and oatmeal bar, got dressed, and had decided to read someone else's *Times* at the coffee shop until I spotted my blue plastic bag at the end of the sidewalk. I think about death a lot now, but not in the mornings when my routine works.

Chapter 11

We first moved to Atlanta in 1973 and right away, I was invited to join a garden club. "Black dirt doesn't go with red nail polish," I replied. A rebuff; but I didn't realize it then. Garden Clubs are more about gossip than dogwoods. Their members worry about property values and infill, about dogs without leashes, and traffic. Ours was not a dead-end street. It soon became a popular short cut. Before Wes died, complaints accelerated and fence control surfaced. New fences are either too high or too thick.

"We must see the street and what's coming next in order to turn," said one woman who has visited the zoning board so often, the members know her full name and address. Remodeling is a critical issue as well. Trucks and mini cement mixers get in the way of Chem Lawn and the UPS truck. Most women work now, but some fill their lives with complaints: *your dog frightened my cat*; and God forbid, if a car is parked on the street two days in a row in the same spot! But here in my new condo, another kind of destruction fills the screen.

The governor of Mississippi came on *The Today Show* at 7:00 a.m. His voice quavered, and there were tears in his eyes. "We will rebuild", he said twice. His wrinkles suggested that he knew what it meant to start over. Matt Lauer looked as serious as I've ever seen him. There's a tornado watch in North Georgia and the sky started out charcoal gray, but now, at l0 a.m., the sun has slipped through the clouds. The power is out in my apartment, but

35

not here; the coffee grinder whirs and its smell finds me. I'm content with *The Times* and yesterday's news within it. In fact, it's good to be away from my TV. The power might just go back on, and I'd find myself switching channels to get five versions of the bad news—Fox, CBS, CNN, CNBC and NBC. It's a surreal alphabetical mess. And the water continues to rise in New Orleans while the politicians argue.

Chapter 12

This morning I looked out the window to see if any rain had fallen, and was surprised to find sunshine; so I took a bathing suit out of my dresser drawer, hurried into it, and walked out the door with a giant towel under my arm. I was in a rush, worried we might catch the New Orleans weather as forecasted. I skipped my stretches and swam to the other side of the pool when, lo and behold, I found a band-aid floating at my side! The pool cleaner is back to work, but he must have slept in today. He was probably glued to the tube past midnight too, because the storm appeared to be creeping toward Georgia and the word "tornado" was mentioned more than once. I didn't waste time thinking about band-aids or sanitary pools. I walked back to my apartment, took a shower, threw on a striped dress and my yellow Huaraches, stuck *The Times* in my purse, and walked on to the coffee shop.

It's Monday and the headlines assaulted me. I forgot about the weather and the walk and pulled the paper closer to my face. The line is long for "Coffee of the Day." It's Hazelnut. The coffee grinder takes the total attention of the girl who runs it.

President Bush is finally touring New Orleans. Last night the lights came on and I sat in front of CNN letting my thoughts roam during the commercials. There stood Anderson Cooper, small, intense, standing up to the wind and rain and to the politicos he interviews. He turned out to be the other son of Gloria Vanderbilt—his brother Carter Cooper jumped out of the family's fourteenth floor apartment after a long conversation with Gloria pleading with him to come off the ledge. She wrote a memoir about him; a thin book and my students loved it. There's a lot more beneath all her face lifts and that starched smile. Anderson Cooper came out of it all, and that's something to be proud of.

"This is life and death," Anderson says, "and the wind rages on. 'There was death all around me,' a forty-four year old man told his rescuer as he hoisted himself into the boat."

Tuesday I stopped reading the paper. I ate a scone and drank a glass of milk, feeling more nutrition might help. Today, the shop is full of earnest folks talking in small groups. There is no line; only a straggler walking through the door every few minutes. The clerks are in the back room, and the September sun enters the floor-to-ceiling windows and warms me up. The regulars all leave tips.

Chapter 13

Ihave always worked with words. First, as a proofreader and, when my eyes got tired, as an English teacher, way past 3:15 p.m. A psychiatrist's wife fares better with a career of her own. At night, like other American husbands, psychiatrists are worn out—eager for a hot meal and relief. It's much better when you don't try to badger them with, "How was your day?" Talk can wait. They can't talk about their patients; ethics get in the way, and they need rest—even sleep, first. They need sustenance, comfort. Sometimes they need a punching bag as well.

After I retired from high school, I bounced around adult education programs at Spelman, Emory, and the Unitarian Church. My editing work has continued, seen through thick lenses now, gradually diminishing from teaching evening classes at Callanwolde Fine Arts Center, to editing the manuscript of the only unpublished student left. I have a feeling that I've told this story before. I'm so proud of it. I think about my students far more than I ever expected to. Their voices. Their high expectations. Their suffering. In the end, I may become no different from any other old woman in a porch rocker bragging about the high points in her life—clinging to whole memories—as their edges blur.

My other students don't need me now. After six years of "The Memoir: Reading It and Writing It," three of them have found small press publishers. One ended up self-publishing his life story about growing up under Castro; and the tall Irishman who memorialized his old neighborhood in Syracuse has moved back there where he is trying to finish what he started. My one elderly student earned a Ragdale Foundation fellowship and moved to Chicago to live with his daughter. So, after attending a signing at Barnes and Noble and the Decatur Library, and drinking my way through two lavish book parties for the small press trio, I was left here sitting in this new living room, staring at the blurbs I wrote for their book covers, warmed by their reflected glory.

Now, on Thursday nights, I arrive early at the coffee shop, order a decaf, and play around with Equal packets until my former student arrives. His name is David Bates, and his is an irregular writing pattern: months of frenzied, late night work; two weeks of writer's block, and now, plodding along, steady and prompt, through computer missteps and thunderstorm power outages. He has six working titles, but he can't settle on one. His life story is full of loss and faith, of mind-numbing poverty and a string of jobs: union organizer, house parent in a home for the retarded, dishwasher in a deli, dog walker and teacher. He quit that one before tenure could make him safe. He's unemployed now and living in a rented room on the Marta bus line with all day and all night to write. Sometimes his one-liners puncture my facade and I cry. Not in front of him, though. He lives on his savings and I worry. What will I do when he finishes his book? I don't dwell on that question. The coffee shop helps me stay in the here and now. As Joan Didion says, "Every day is all there is."

I stick close to home with the exception of my walk to the branch library every three weeks. It's more than a mile, and I take my time. Often, I doze in a recliner there and read *The New Yorker* before I walk back. There's a brick wall I lean on, if I get tired. It surrounds one of those McMansions still for sale. Why should I hurry? I know about naps sitting up in a recliner and in a bed; even naps on the bus, but not on purpose. Age makes you parcel out your energy. I can't run any longer, to be sure. In fact, my so-called running costume went to Goodwill when Wes died. And this summer, for too many days the heat has kept me indoors looking out of a window that faces the swimming pool. I miss watching that dragonfly, the one that circles the water and disappears into the willow tree at the pool's edge. The dragon fly has outlasted its comrades who float on the surface until the pool boy captures them in his net, but I've already told you that part of my story.

Chapter 14

Disaster seeps into the very air we breathe. Now the news is full of terror threats on the New York subway. The sky is full of rain clouds. I heard a chilling story at the coffee shop this week about childhood and Christmas. Three women, the third being me, were talking about the holiday. There was a pause between the mention of Christmas and the first woman's voice. She owns a ranch in Texas—she's an old fashioned liberal who graduated from Oberlin.

The rancher asked: "Do you know those silver Christmas trees that were popular for a while?"

Everyone nodded. "Ours spun around. A colored light was aimed at it."

"Didn't it have ornaments?" I asked.

"It did not." The owner of the ranch moved her napkin to the right and blew her nose.

Then the conversation switched to what was under our trees. I was eager to tell my story. "I always had a pile of gifts, even if they were cheap. Picture frames and underwear from Kresge's. Raisinettes from movie theaters. Key chains advertising car dealerships. I loved Christmas. I depended on it. When I was seven, a bossy girl at school insisted that there was no Santa Claus. Then my mother told me the whole truth; whereupon I had a tantrum on her bed. I couldn't stop crying, and I refused to climb under that faded chenille spread. In the morning, it was raining hard and I woke up before breakfast."

The second woman asked the Texas rancher what she got for Christmas: "We all got stock certificates in long envelopes laid on the carpet under our silver tree."

"No toys?" everyone said at once, and the rancher shook her head.

The third woman said: "We had a pile of toys, and I'm Jewish. We celebrated both holidays. Maybe my father wanted to assimilate!"

Everyone sort of chuckled. The image of that cold silver tree and four small children was slow to materialize. We seemed lost in thought trying to imagine what our responses would have been. Would we have torn up the envelope in anger? Would we have cried? Would we have remained still and watched our parents until someone said something? The silver imagery revealed something to me that can't be put into words. Conversations like this one are rare at the coffee shop. I finally stopped listening to these disillusioned women and thought about Wes and our first Christmas together, and then our last one:

That first Christmas, Wes and I had temporary jobs at a new boutique across the street from our apartment building. After Thanksgiving, business increased and so did our hours; sometimes ending as late as 9:30 in the evening. Imagine how happy we were when the owner asked Wes to shovel snow and both of us to advance from sales to looking out for shoplifters—a real problem with all the small, high priced ornaments crammed up against imported glass from Mexico and Swedish toy trains. So I became a spy of sorts and Wes added physical labor, out in the elements, sweeping and shoveling early and late.

I've never had a job where I felt so appreciated. The owner was thrilled to find his business booming and even happier when we jumped at the chance to work longer hours and weren't afraid to confront thieves. We rushed to work, ate sandwiches on the run, and saved our paychecks. Why concern ourselves with a broken elevator, an occasional roach, or a hard-to-find caretaker? Everything we wanted, for the moment, waited in those two buildings. In another year, we might have encountered serious snow drifts, a lingering recession, or the kind of bronchitis that won't let up. But that year we watched the owner pour Polish vodka and an entire bottle of grenadine syrup over a block of ice in the pottery punch bowl he still hoped to sell for 50 dollars. It was Christmas Eve, an hour before closing. Snow dusted the sidewalks and continued falling. The fruitcake was gone, and the punch reduced to pink residue, when a perennial grad student well known in the neighborhood, pulled out a fifth of Jameson and passed it around to the staff. We wished him well, said goodbye to the owner, who was resting in the single Arne Jacobsen chair he had moved from the back room, and left with the snow shovel and key. Outside the snow now melted before it hit the ground and felt like rain on our coats.

Our Christmas goose, now defrosted, waited on the kitchen table near a five pound sack of potatoes and a can of English peas. Wes returned it to the refrigerator, and we sat on the couch watching the snow fall into the courtyard, three floors below. I looked up, eventually, to see Wes, his eyes closed, still ramrod straight, as if they were open. A long standing habit, it became—of pushing himself to the limit—never considering a nap—and in that final year we had together, no longer straight, but leaning a little to the side, asleep.

Our final Christmas was an exercise in leftovers: instead of a tree, red ornaments we'd kept for 30 years piled in a silver bowl, love-notes to each other instead of presents, and two Cornish game hens instead of a turkey. We poured bourbon over crushed ice and watched as that gadget on the refrigerator rushed the ice particles into our old fashioned glasses. We rested, on and off, all day and played "I'll Have a Blue Christmas Without You," too many times. Elvis passed me by in college, but his voice and legend have surfaced at odd moments since. My favorite is "That's Alright, Mama." PBS replays one of his concerts from time to time. There he stands in that silly white jump suit with his leg moving up and down and sweat pouring from his face. Wes and I fell asleep in chairs that Christmas afternoon. We drifted off in the middle of what might have been nostalgia, but we held onto each other all night long—rearranging ourselves each time one of us got up to go to the bathroom—my legs grasping his, as if it mattered, as if it could save him and us.

Chapter 15

Pain makes me think I'll be content with anything but it, and for a while I am content. I stay in bed on my back. I'm reluctant to move. I wait to shut the bedroom door, to turn off the TV in the next room, or to use the toilet. I limit my movements to pressing the buttons on the remote. After all, it doesn't take long to synchronize the channels, and I try to remember the famous women who became addicted to pain medication. It's a long list, but Elizabeth Taylor and President Ford's wife stand out. The Betty Ford Clinic is still in business and Taylor has spent time there.

What still occupies my mind is that little pain that remains after the white pill vanishes in a gulp of water, and how short the hours seem when the pills are gone and I am left with the image of my spinal cord on the films that the doctor slapped on the wall.

"A bulging disc that hits a nerve," the doctor continued.

"You have choices," he added. "A cortisone shot? A Chiropractor? Surgery? Or Acupuncture? There are no guarantees."

"I'll take cortisone." I didn't waver – even after he said it doesn't work on everyone.

"You'll have to stay off your blood thinner for a week."

"What will happen to me if I stop taking blood thinners?"

"It is a matter of percentages." The doctor sat down. I wanted to ask for a refill, but I didn't.

"I'm sure it is. Surgery has risks. Chiropractors are quacks, and I'm even more skeptical of all those acupuncture needles!" So the doctor handed me an appointment card and helped me off the examining table.

Chapter 16

Two men came in the coffee shop today, loud and deep in a conversation about abortion. CNN now alternates the faces of Harriet Miers and some guy from Kansas who wants her off the ticket because she's able to change her mind. The loud men pulled me away from thinking about the Today Show or going on any further with *The New York Times*. The taller of the two was the most obnoxious and, as he bent forward, he was almost face to face with the other man: "Listen, fool, I had a sister who wasn't lucky enough to even hear the words *Roe* and *Wade*. She went off to college to study voice and piano. And when the music director told her, 'If you were a little more accommodating, you could be the star of the show,' she took him seriously. Well, she became the star; and when the show was over and the semester too, she went to one of those doctors in a white frame house off campus. His medical license had been pulled, so the story went. The music director and the doctor had warned her about the law, so she dialed the doctor who evidently had left the little white house by then. She was too scared to go to the ER when she started to hemorrhage. She must have fainted because I found her that evening with the phone near her hand on a bloodied carpet. No more music for my sister then. I didn't even know she was pregnant until the day before. I leaned against that kitchen countertop thinking: we aren't powerful people and I wasn't raised to use my fists, so there is nothing legal to be done here. Nothing."

Then the first man stopped talking. The other man was quiet too, looking down at the tea bag wrapped around his spoon. I'm sure he wasn't expecting this slice of life. "I'm sorry," he offered. Then the dead girl's brother kept on, but his voice was lower and his anguish had been changed to an academic posture: "They really did use knitting needles in the projects where immigrants filled up the apartments, in the days when another mouth to feed meant someone else wouldn't get fed."

I walked to the bathroom at this point and splashed water on my face. I had my own abortion story; but you wouldn't catch me telling it in public or private, for that matter. Only Wes knew. I told him everything before we got married.

Chapter 17

Not infrequently, two women come in the shop and take seats near the counter where I have staked out a place for myself and where I try to keep the seat beside me open for Bachner. It's silly to generalize, and I'm not reaching for scientific examples of talking styles; but there is usually a talker and a listener rather than an even exchange; and the woman talking is intense, sometimes shrill. That's the way it was this morning. Loud enough for me to hear. Loud enough for the men with cell phones to glance away from the papers in front of them or to move a file folder aside. Bachner never appeared, so I left in the middle of the loud words.

This afternoon I came back. I slipped onto my stool and eavesdropped on two social workers in the brown leather corner chairs, the most comfortable chairs in the shop; even better than the overstuffed sofa in the back. The listener leaned on her elbow with her hand covering half her mouth and hardly moved. It was impossible to tell her reaction by just glancing at her eyes. The subject was Indians. From India. Still hoping to see Bachner, I kept glancing at the door.

"If I was the administrator, he'd be gone in five minutes. This is a university town and computer people are a dime a dozen. You can't tell me that it's faulty machines. And I don't care if they called him every day of his vacation. If he'd done his job in the first place, they wouldn't have to call him!"

The woman looked in a state of collapse herself: one of those almost shaved heads that look good only if you have a pretty face. Her haircut had grown out, revealing cowlicks no hairbrush could fix. She was dressed for the weather, which has turned cold again; but her scarf was faded and her coat was missing a button.

"They're liars anyway. Didn't that guy you met, the one on a diet, tell you that *those people* will say anything just to keep you in their Indian restaurants, even upscale ones, where curry mixtures are full of salt and sugar and have grease floating on the top, yet they would insist that such a mess is low cal? And, I don't care if he went to Oxford University; he probably majored in English Literature instead of computer science. His British accent doesn't impress me either. And if they add one more family to my case load, I'm quitting. I'd rather be painting bathrooms than be immersed in squalor with all *those people*. You can thank God you're working out of the office, Mary Virginia!"

I sat there thinking about *those people*. Are *those people* akin to you people? Probably. The Department of Children and Family Services here has a hard time spotting endangered children. Last year, more than one of them turned up dead: either tied to a bed post or weighing 60 pounds and asleep on a gray sheet with a thin blanket pulled up to their necks. There's a feature writer for the *Atlanta Journal-Constitution* who grabs up details like those and slaps them on the page so that the power of such neglect can make a person shake. The social worker today in the coffee shop makes me sick to my stomach. I can't finish my muffin, and walnut orange is my favorite. It lies broken in the saucer, and I am left with a fantasy where I cram the muffin into the big talker's mouth and watch the crumbs part company.

Eventually, I leave the shop, walk to Publix and buy four pairs of black tights. They hide the blue veins in my legs. Besides, colder weather is coming. Then I come back to my place on the coffee shop stool, and I'll be damned if the two social workers are not still talking. I don't dare order a second muffin.

"And what's more, I'm sick of them taking over every Dairy Queen in town! And don't hand me that crap about Ghandi being a hero!"

Chapter 18

The last time Wes and I flew to New Orleans we didn't do much. I slept late while Wes spent his mornings at meetings about stalkers and cults. I learned some details from him that were eye-openers, like the methods suggested to disarm a stalker: never change your phone number; instead, install an answering machine recorder on the line so that the stalker's messages can be captured. Then get a new phone number and only give it out to a few trusted friends. "Why?" I asked. Wes just accepted the forensic psychiatrist's advice without question. "I've forgotten most of it," he said, "But the main point was never getting into another conversation with a stalker." Sounds like common sense to me, I thought.

"Cults are another matter. The Church of Scientology is a cult, and some big Hollywood names are true believers. Apparently one of their leaders was an involuntary patient in a psychiatric hospital himself, and from that experience, he grew to hate psychiatry and psychiatrists. There's a frightening, mind-control aspect to scientology. I forget exactly how its leaders collected compromising data on members of the movement, but they used their information to try to prevent anyone from breaking away."

I stopped listening to Wes at this point and thought about the low buildings in the French Quarter, and the old men in the street leaning forward to listen to a corner saxophone player. I wanted to learn more about its history. I am still in love with the city and a weekend there seemed like the honeymoon we wished we'd had. We ate fresh seafood for four days; and after supper, we walked past closed antique shops and into used book stores. There were seven of them in the Quarter. My favorite had two walls filled with French books. The owner's business card was twice the size of an ordinary one with pale gray engraving. The sofas there were old and overstuffed. I hated to leave, but we ambled down the street holding hands. We ate ice cream cones at a corner bar attached to our hotel. Then we walked through the Ritz lobby next door and sunk into the couches there. Sometimes we took the trolley to the Café du Monde and absorbed the night together. Sugar from the beignets sweetened our fingers. I didn't want to leave the café or the city.

Today a burning building collapsed in downtown New Orleans; and the mayor came on TV. He looked both lost and enraged, if that's possible. "Some of the people you have come to help are already dead," he said. Yet neither the mayor nor the Governor nor the President is the hero of this disaster. The policemen who have been wading in shit for days, without sleep, knowing their own homes are ruined, the officers who didn't turn their guns on themselves, who didn't run with the loot; those policemen stand tall in my book. Meanwhile fires still burn in the shops on Canal Street and in warehouses along the waterfront. I fell asleep last night dreaming of New Orleans and Wes and the past. It was a dream full of pleasure and fresh air. I woke up to the sound of a horse in the morning sun, his hooves on the cobblestone. The dream receded and I closed my eyes hoping for another one.

The year before I met Wes, I was drinking Cutty Sark and eating peanuts in one of those cheap canvas chairs that grad students bought back in 1962. Butterfly chairs. The party was an after work thing on a Friday night following a week of overtime and snow plows. It began with happy hour at the bar on the first floor of the office building where I was a proofreader. My best friend that year was a philosophy major who never finished her degree but who could out-talk any PhD candidate in the field. She was working part-time with me and looking for something more substantial in her off hours. She had married a *ne'er do well* who treated her like window dressing. She looked better in the requisite little black dress than any girl I ever knew and he snapped her up before she had a chance to think straight, lighting her cigarettes and promising her plenty of time to finish her dissertation.

She eventually discovered that he was all show. He bought Sartre's collected works in hardcover, but never cracked a volume. He hoarded recordings of Chet Baker when everyone else was drawn to Motown. He invited what he thought were campus movers and shakers to his parties and served beef stroganoff when our other friends could barely afford macaroni and cheese. In the meantime, my friend stood in doorways wearing a denim shirtwaist with a cigarette in her hand—smoking her way through his evenings—watching us all. He emptied her ash trays and overlooked her silences.

I always had the feeling there was a little voice safe inside my friend whispering, "I'm here to observe." Yet she was no gossip. She had spent the summer after her sophomore year touring Europe with a guy she met on the boat. He bought a used motorcycle, and they lived on bread and cheese so totally that she had scurvy when she returned to campus in the fall. I loved to listen to her stories about that stolen summer. Even youth hostels outside Copenhagen seemed exotic to me then. I hung out in their apartment too much, eating dinner there more often than not, listening to Eartha Kitt on their radio, dreaming about the day when I might be under the bridges of Paris with a stranger. My friend seemed like a woman of the world and I trusted her judgment.

She was enchanted by a trumpet player who lived across the hall, and I accepted her first impression as if it was a philosophical premise that we had memorized for a midterm. This musician was a quiet man, unlike her husband, and she had read more into his pauses than was ever there. Suffice it to say that I walked across the hall one night after a party, and he introduced me to oral sex. I would have been okay, if I had stuck with it. But, at heart, I am a conventional person and two months later I realized I was pregnant. He never knew. I borrowed $200 for an abortion from the father of a gay friend and repaid it at $10 a week. In the end, I got a long letter with a list of the payments, their dates, and a short tribute to my character. Years later, my gay friend told me that his father knew what his money was being used for all along. By then, my shame had dissipated along with my rage. But I have never stopped being grateful.

Chapter 19

I've had to forsake my cronies in the coffee shop for the last few weeks to rest. The flu season is upon us, so I got my shot at Publix with my Medicare card without having to stand in line. Yet here I am with the flu and homemade cough syrup in a teapot at my bedside: lemon slices, honey, and enough whiskey to reach the top. I slept so long I almost burned up the chicken soup left on simmer. I slept right through the TV hoopla about Harriet Miers. This morning *The Today Show* profiled Bush's new pick; a man with a solid résumé, big brains, and lifelong conservative credentials. There is no doubt in anyone's mind where this Supreme Court nominee stands on abortion.

Propaganda for the war and against it continues. And now the army is in the hands of a better public relations agency with restrained graphic design and clever words. Yet a lone voice rises up and takes its place in my mind beside Ralph Waldo Emerson: "Whoso would be a man must be a non-conformist." Who are the examples from history? Jesus, Socrates, Galileo? I try to remember who said, "Power corrupts; and absolute power corrupts absolutely." I can't. Am I just an old woman still trying to make sense of my high school American literature and history lessons? Or are Tim Russert and Chris Matthews the honorable men here? For once, I'm not sure. The mayor of New Orleans turned out to be a fool. And I gave him every benefit of every doubt. Where is the truth to be found in this political quagmire?

I haven't seen so much fire on my TV screen since the summer Detroit and Newark burned in a surreal landscape of rocks and bottles. Shabby neighborhood stores formed a backdrop for the frenzied looting that followed those riots. The fires in France make me wonder what is really happening now. It is no longer summer in Atlanta, and I haven't bothered to find out what the weather in Paris has to do with anything. In the meantime, cars burn in Parisian suburbs and riots break out in a string of cities far up the coast of Normandy. Skeletons of torched automobiles fill the evening news and the morning reports. The total, well past 3,000 cars on the twelfth day of the carnage, accumulates in spite of a curfew which has slowed things down some.

The headlines this morning reveal that Chirac, lover of the spotlight, has retreated from the flames and waits somewhere while a spokesman mouths his words. The interior minister, Nicolas Sarkozy, was applauded in Parliament when he called for swift deportations of legal and illegal immigrants caught in the act, so to speak. The Internet is supposed to account for this swift spread of destruction; but gradually a few facts leak out of the sound bites on TV that I hope will explain what I call revolution, not *unrest*. The strangest fact is that only a few people have been killed.

Here in the coffee shop, Bachner is nowhere to be found, and the man whose divorce is in its final stages is reading the Bible now. The car pool mothers are talking about a bake sale and trading recipes with the owner's wife. Last weekend a tornado swept aside a trailer park in Indiana until the ground was covered in sticks; and through it all, I tried to concentrate on Chirac. He had a stroke last year too; and I wonder if his retreat has to do with fear of another one. The very word *stroke* causes me to step gingerly, looking at the sidewalks for cracks, watching for cars so carefully that a teenager covered in gothic black admonished me: "Hurry up, lady. It's all clear." I step forward slowly. I continue, still watching my feet, and eventually arrive safe inside my apartment.

It would be easy to hole up behind these closed doors with Amazon.com instead of the public library, with Netflicks and new magazine subscriptions instead of the coffee shop. I could rely on delivery boys and live in my sweats. In fact, it would be easier still to spend the winter in fleece pajamas ordering Christmas baskets to be sent, wrapped, to the few acquaintances I have left and, of course, to Bachner. But I have rarely taken the easy way out, so I won't start now.

Chapter 20

I was in such a fog this morning that I forgot it was Sunday until I saw the fat edition of the *Times*. There it was at my door, and I hadn't even heard the thud. I didn't have the strength to pick it up before my coffee, so I kicked it inside and found my way to the coffee shop. Everything is different on Sunday. Not one barista to recognize me or to know I still had a cup on the shelf behind the grinder with my name on it. In some ways, being anonymous is a relief. Today I surrendered to the words floating around me. Two women were talking at a rapid rate.

"Where's the bitch?' I said to her." The first woman had a raspy voice.

"You got kicked out over saying that?" Her companion looked both startled and nervous.

"Well, the bitch was sitting right behind the plants; no, not sitting, bent over." The woman drained her coffee cup.

"You didn't protest when they canceled you out?" Her companion began to attract attention as her voice rose in volume.

"Well, they gave me my money back; and I had paid for a full year *with* towels."

"I still can't believe there wasn't more to it. You're just looking for excuses. You'll never find an exercise club so convenient to your house. With a pool, already."

These two women didn't stay long, and not a minute went by before a tall girl with crutches and a big purse entered. She sat down near the door, and without a word, the barista brought over a bigger than usual pumpkin muffin with loose raisins spilling forth. I considered getting one myself, but I waited. Next came a disheveled matron with her head in the air and a grimace to match. She coughed. Not a full fledged cough; nothing matched her red nose and sunken eyes.

She sat down next to me and didn't order a thing. "Did you break your leg?" She looked at the first woman and her muffin and responded haltingly: "Yes, I broke it playing nose tackle for the USC football team." Now the barista began to cough in earnest. Her cough didn't sound authentic either.

"What's a nose tackle?" the girl who couldn't decide what to order wouldn't let it rest.

"I don't know. I just made that up. My leg isn't broken. I have Lupus."

Thank goodness that revelation shut everybody up.

"Can't you see I'm ready for a latté?" said one of the regulars. The barista took her time making one; and when she was finished, the phone rang and she answered it. The day was starting to take on a better direction. Maybe I'll call Bachner and ask if he can find an egg white omelet somewhere. The coffee shop is full now. Every chair is taken and the line is long. I continue to listen. Voices come from the back of the shop. I can't see who's talking there, and wiping off my eyeglasses doesn't help.

"Being a clown must put you in the thick of life."

"Hardly. It's just standin' around acting dumb."

"How long did you have to go to school for that?"

"I thought I'd make money on the side, but word of mouth didn't get me very far. With the gas crisis and all, most kids around here are happy to blow out some candles fast and open their presents. What I need is an agent and a better neighborhood."

"You never answered my question. How long did you go to school?"

I leave in the middle of this exchange before I can attach faces to the voices. I'm walking back. Bachner doesn't answer his cell, so I'll have to be satisfied with the muffins I'm bringing home with me.

Chapter 21

The noise of a leaf blower assaulted me as I shut my door this morning and became louder as I passed a red maple at the gate of the apartment complex. I walked fast to escape the sound. Bachner was back on his stool looking glum, so I left him to his thoughts. I just sat down and nodded, my feet tucked safely into the rungs of the stool.

Bachner reads *The New York Times* on line, so he already knew the fires had reached Paris; and a list of numbers came from his mouth in a flat staccato rhythm. I pictured the burning cars, the smoke. The woman next to him dipped a cinnamon roll in her coffee-to-go cup. Soon she left and he turned to me: "Well, You can kiss Paris goodbye," he said.

I smiled, thinking of a party Wes and I gave back in the days when our guests drank until dawn and then stayed for breakfast: Calvados and Pernod, Hemingway drinks, part of his moveable feast at our table in the glare of morning. All we knew of Paris then came from those early novels. As usual, the sound of the coffee maker brought me from the memory of those parties to what lies in front of me here—a single bran muffin. I've already kissed Paris goodbye along with any hope of walks near bookshops and the Tuileries. Soon I'll need a wheelchair to navigate the streets, if I should ever be fortunate enough to go.

Next, I opened the paper and read the headline: "French Officials Try to Ease Fear as Crisis Swells: Curfews and Extra Police Officers Planned."

"What happens next?" I thought then and now. I keep thinking of those 60's fires. Again and again, the images float through my head. They overlap the here and now. I'll never forget them.

Buildings and cars burned, but rocks and bottles were the modus operandi of the urban desperate in 1967—rocks, bottles and whatever was at hand those summers when people sat on their stoops and hate festered. Summer in the north was an explosion then; but it is no longer summer in Atlanta, and the only red and gold here is attached to the trees. Can it still be summer in France? I planned to ask Bachner, but he hasn't been back from Amsterdam long enough to unpack his bags.

One thousand cars on fire, and now the rate has accelerated! I saw a shot of the Arch de Triumph last night when I turned off the television sound so I could sleep. Did they shoot holes in gas tanks and throw in matches? With all those explosions, why has no one died? Are they torching cars in rich neighborhoods too? Nothing makes sense to me on day twelve of these riots. When does a riot become a revolution? My dreams are full of stick figures floating in puddles of gasoline—falling out of picture frames.

The weather here, miserable now for a whole week, shows no sign of letting up; and conversation at the coffee shop reflects the temperature.

"You need a fireplace in here." The divorced man came in early today. "One of those electric ones; they're cheaper." Nobody laughed.

"How cheap?" Bachner is back at last.

What do you want; the exact amount, tax included?"

Their banter is drowned out by a hot argument over Dick Cheney's hidden plans and the subject of torture. Katie Couric was interviewed by an interrogator who was as soft spoken and diplomatic a man as I've ever seen on early morning TV. It seemed as if she should be interviewing him. I couldn't concentrate. I paid more attention to her ruffled blouse than anything they said. I have the attention span of a moth!

Yesterday, Marilyn Minter's "Stepping Up," a painting on metal that explores the seedy side of glamour almost filled the first page of the Arts Section of the *Times*. I was so rattled by the image of a dirty human heel in a backless, heavily jeweled stiletto that I kept returning to the page to look at it. Scary thoughts filled my head and dishes stayed in my sink. It was only a photo in the *Times*, but I couldn't let it be. Finally, I cut it out and used it for a bookmark.

Then the phone rang. Bachner and I are planning a birthday party for Max Beale. He'll be 70 next week. We can't decide where to have it. I want it in my apartment, but Bachner says the work will be too much for me. "What work?" I say, "You pick up a few things at Costco and I'll iron my dinner napkins and make potato soup." We struck a bargain finally. I busied myself making a grocery list while he promised to clean up afterwards. "I'll bring garbage bags: the white ones with red ties, and we'll need paper plates." Bachner likes to talk about details. I hung up the phone and returned to the television.

The TV screen is full of smashed lumber and New Orleans residents with their heads down. "This is your whole life. There it is—in a pile." The rowboats and newscasters are gone, and at night they are rerunning Ken Burns' history of Jazz. I fell asleep to early Louis Armstrong and woke up to *Stormy Weather.* Lena Horne's voice is some consolation.

This morning at the coffee shop one voice rose above the others. "She's an ugly, vicious toad and one day I'm going to tell her how the cow eats the corn!" The woman was very carefully *turned out,* as we said in the sixties.

"Where are you from?" replied an equally fashionable lady.

"Charleston. But you don't have to live on a farm to know what goes on there."

"Whatever did the toad say to you?"

"She told everyone in my office that I was a lesbian. You know how *born-agains* feel about homosexuals—I could get fired. My boss takes *the rapture* seriously!"

"I didn't realize you were gay."

"I'm not gay. Just sour on marriage after my husband ran away with our travel agent and moved to Canada. In fact, I'm thinking about moving in with Jackson and putting my furniture in storage. You can get plastic containers to organize most anything, and I've already surrendered a U-Haul full of leftovers that has traveled all the way to Vancouver. My ex-husband's a *filmmaker,* you know."

"A filmmaker? In Vancouver?"

"Yeah. He earns a living now, but I had to work a fifty hour week if I wanted a car of my own and a wardrobe that didn't come from Goodwill. Anyway, he accused me of plenty, but loving women was not part it."

The bitter divorcee ordered some pumpkin concoction they're touting for the holidays and a cranberry muffin as an afterthought. I watched her take her time with both as her friend talked on about movies: the pace of "Shop Girl" and why "Chicken Little" was too violent for her niece. Suddenly, the topic switched to spas.

"I came out looking like I was covered in pig shit!" The divorcee's voice caught the attention of everyone at the counter.

"Was it refreshing?" I asked, listening to an endless tale about mud baths at a retreat in the Carolina mountains and hoping for a response to my sarcasm.

"They hike there, but you have to be careful going down hills. The leaves are gone from those trees too, and they left in September." She ignored me.

Bachner offered to loan me some videos. Anne Bancroft movies never disappoint me: *The Graduate, Agnes of God, Home for the Holidays*, (hard to remember it is Thanksgiving; not Christmas), the one about the book lover during World War II. Bancroft always brings the best actors in with her: Jane Fonda, Holly Hunter, Dustin Hoffman, the Englishman who portrayed a monster in *Silence of the Lambs*, the list only stops because my memory grows weak. Bachner's collection must be something. I've never seen his place or his books. He brought me these movies in a Whole Foods bag with a handle.

Instead of watching Bancroft last night, I sat back in my recliner and observed Caroline Schlossberg hand out performance awards at the Kennedy Center. Julie Harris, Tina Turner and Robert Redford sat side by side, intent. I wanted to crawl in the tube and sit beside them leaving my fiery dreams behind. They looked so old and so happy. Sun has damaged Redford, and Julie Harris does nothing to hide her arthritic fingers. So very old. Stalwarts— all of them.

I have all the time in the world left to watch Anne Bancroft. Or do I?

Chapter 22

The political scene in the coffee shop has some ins and outs. Some stops and starts. Today a woman walked in hoping for an exotic tea. I wasn't paying attention to the tea because I saw her shirt with an American flag and a message on the front and was trying to read the message on the back; but she moved, and the line grew long with only a few spaces to peek through. "Learn to speak English" was the admonition on the front. Finally, I asked her what was on the back as I made my way to the toilet. "It says the same thing in Spanish, Vietnamese, and Arabic!" I kept walking, but I did smile. What a hypocrite I am! I wanted to ask, "How many foreign languages do you speak?" But it seemed too tame a question and I didn't think of that response until I was washing my hands. I let the warm water run and paid attention to the graphics on the wall, "Barista Wanted."

There are tornado warnings in North Georgia, and already the shelves at Publix are cleared of white bread. Things are bad in Kentucky and Tennessee too. I missed the *Today Show,* but everyone at the coffee shop is talking about the weather, even a cop. "How could I know for sure what's coming?" he smiles to the woman ahead of him in line: "I already have my sack full of emergency supplies under my stool, and I am about to order a pound of French roast, just in case." He leaves a dollar for the waitress.

Two much older men put all this talk of the weather in a back seat: "The guy was fishing and a storm came up. There was a bad waterspout, and he was hit by a bass."

"What's a waterspout?" replied the younger man.

"He's a substitute teacher who doesn't go in every day," explained the fisherman to anyone who would listen. The fisherman takes a fatherly approach to the younger man.

"It is a small tornado over the water."

"A bass? Where was this?"

"Somewhere near Mrytle Beach—the Little River Inlet."

"Why haven't I heard of a waterspout before?" the substitute teacher couldn't be that interested in fishing, I thought. You can tell he admires the older man. Bachner does too.

"They're actually common, but most people don't get hit by a bass!"

I bury myself in *The Times* and wait for Bachner. Finally I leave and as I am about to shut my apartment door, I hear my new neighbor's voice. I listen to her for a long time, standing still. My neighbor is southern. Grew up here and went to school here too—Agnes Scott. She didn't tell me this; I asked to see her photo albums, and there she was in her graduation dress and white gloves; a good looking woman. "It's time to use the good china," she said a month later as I dropped off a cold supper from Publix. Here in the South, dinner still means something, even if it's cold. She lingered at her door, talking about the ingredients for a long time. Today she invited me in for coffee, and I accepted even though it was my third cup. I can only guess how lonely she must be now that her glory days are over.

Mint grows in a flower pot on her kitchen table. She keeps casseroles in the freezer for emergencies. The emergencies turn out to be funerals. She may lie about her age or have nothing but older friends. I'm not sure. But I figured out her metaphor. "The good china" means death is in the air. *This heat is deadly for women as old as we are.* And every night someone on TV warns against staying out in the noonday sun. They needn't worry about me. I head straight for my bed; and, despite all that caffeine, fall asleep.

A plane crashed in Greece and right away there was talk of Al Qaeda. It hasn't been that long since the subway bombings in London, and everyone is on edge. This morning a husband shot his elderly wife in the intensive care unit at St. Joseph's Hospital; then shot himself. Bachner is at Hilton Head this week sitting Shiva with a friend. I try to focus on the flowers that some neighborhood group planted at the entrances to the freeway. They didn't just toss wildflower seeds in the air. Someone designed the plantings. Every morning, Mexican workers walk past the flowers on their way to the Shell station where they hope to be picked up for a day of labor. By noon, the leftover men pass by the flowers again on their way back to some unknown place. It is not uncommon for six of them to share one small bedroom, so Bachner says. Being a landlord puts him in the thick of things. I never quiz him, but he knows plenty.

Today the coffee grinder and a balladeer compete. Four women line up their morning plans. It's the first day of kindergarten. The women are loud with relief, their sandals tapping nervously under the table they share.

Once in a while a woman comes into the coffee shop who is so robust and full of life that heads turn. Last Friday, it was a teacher in a red skirt. "I teach ballroom dancing," she said to no one in particular. Right away two men came up with a movie title to make sure the conversation didn't end there. The movie was playing at an art theatre in Midtown, and it was a documentary about a contest in the New York school system for ballroom dancing. "Oh, I've seen that documentary twice!" she fairly sparkled. By the time her orange juice was paid for, three other men had stayed long enough to have their coffees refilled.

The word "Mexican" slips from somebody's lips. It is not attached to anything, not even that blast of yellow flowers near the freeway; but when I go home, I see Mexicans and three police cars across the street at the Shell station. If the police and employers in their trucks know the Mexican workers are illegal, why don't they arrest them? There are lawns around here to mow, and the sound of weed-whackers is part of weekend noise. The Mexicans are eager for such seasonal work. Winter is short in Atlanta, just a few rainy, cold weeks between January and the last week of February when the daffodils bloom again.

Today we learned the Manhattan subway scare was a false alarm. Between natural disasters and homemade bombs, our fingers are cold with fear. More hurricanes threaten the Florida Keys. Even New Hampshire is not safe, and the Jersey shore is under water. Bachner left this morning to tend to his mother there. A new set of drawings appeared on the wall in the back of the shop; minimalist, colorful, and all framed in bamboo. Rain fell all afternoon and there has been a run on espresso.

Chapter 23

I remember the last time the Bradford pears bloomed early. All along the freeway like sentinels. It was the spring I began collecting membership cards: one from the local Democratic Party, another from the Southern Poverty Law Center in Montgomery (I joined when the militia threat in Georgia was on the rise, only to find the militia was strongest in Mississippi and Michigan.) I also collected a red, white, and blue piece of plastic from Costco. The photograph on that card made me look like a corpse; but it was Wes who was dying, and he looked healthy.

Opening the mail in the late afternoons that April (the mailman drank, and the mail rarely arrived before suppertime) meant sorting through catalogues, requests for donations and fast food coupons. Usually there was little left but medical bills and insurance forms. They sat unopened in a wire basket on top of our file drawers. The library windows were open and the screens were in place; and I had time to consider the pleasures that were slipping away. Email has almost destroyed the ritual of walking to the mail box. Once in awhile, there's a thank you card or an invitation to a wedding shower we can't attend. I used to give bridal showers, afternoon affairs with a liquor punch and a bowl of berries. The best one was just eight women at my dining room table bringing lingerie for the bride plus a love poem on a card. The shower lasted past dinner time; and the bride told four years later: "People are still talking about that afternoon. And I'm still wearing those black lace brassieres!"

This March I have already spotted a purple crocus, a scrawny daffodil, and now the redbud is breaking out. Since I no longer drive, the Bradford pears are a thing of the past for me. A union rep came into the coffee shop today. She's never heard of Walter Reuther and thinks Jimmy Hoffa was a great man put in prison by bad guys. She wore one of those pin stripe suits you see on a Saks mannequin and it fit. I once dated an older man in college who had his pin stripe shirts custom made. I listened in awe while he told me how important the fit was. He was wearing no shirt at the time. Anyway, I'll bet the union rep's pin stripe cost a fortune and was altered by Mr. Kim on Cheshire Bridge Road. He did all the work for Saks when I shopped there. The union rep was tall and wore boots polished to a fare-thee-well, black like her leather handbag. Saul says she has degrees from N.Y.U. Don't they teach American history anymore? I dared not ask about John L. Lewis and his mine workers.

Walter Reuther was considered the most dangerous man in Detroit. The goons from Ford Motor tried to kill him, more than once; and he eventually moved out to Rochester and lived behind an electric fence. I thought of all those Labor Day parades, his red hair in the wind. They say that Hoffa ran the Teamsters Union from his prison cell; a thug of the first order. I want to believe in unions. I want to believe in a lot of things. I want to believe this union rep is more than a pretty face in an expensive suit. I want to loan her a biography of Reuther, but the 50 year difference in our ages makes me seem closer to an old fool than a wise elder. I should do something. I should send more money to the Democratic Party, but their pleas pile up on my desk. And when I leave the coffee shop I get lost in these useless thoughts. My roommate at Bowling Green University was from Detroit, and she couldn't stop talking about car parts and black lunch pails and how much more her father deserved than he got.

Maybe things will get better when the pool opens. Right now the owners are expanding the apartments straight in back, and I can smell garbage from the Chinese Take Out in the sewer as I walk up the hill. I'm using a cane now and last night I stopped to talk to a guy who says someone has a pit bull in The Cliffs, so he just might get a piece of pipe and have rubber tips slipped on both ends. This guy has a lot of confidence in his aim! Imagine missing the head of that animal and then having it lock its jaw into you! Next I ran into the chocolate brown standard poodle without a leash. As big as a horse, clipped too. They bring the dog shampoo van right to your door in this apartment complex. Rumor has it that a local vet pays house calls too—for a price. I don't believe everything I hear, but the rules here have certainly relaxed!

Chapter 24

Age finds us all eventually whether our choices are many or few. Lauren Bacall had two husbands, three children, and *work* then and now; but it is her dog that brings her comfort at this stage of her life: trained, clean, loyal and worth the price of dog walkers, groomers, and sitters. I've read her two memoirs, but decided not to use them for my class. She didn't use a ghost writer, though. Jane Fonda is having a hip replaced and she doesn't exercise anymore, or so she says. She has had a face lift, and she did get a divorce from Ted Turner as well, though she stayed in Atlanta. So much for celebrities.

Age certainly found me. Before I retreated to this apartment on Shallowford Road, I noticed a big difference in the reactions of strangers. Dapper middle aged men plus men in work boots and tee shirts got up in a hurry in the back of the airport train reserved for the elderly when I walked through the sliding door. Not so with groups of teen age girls who seemed lost in their loud words. Once when I reached up to shake hands with a patron in the library, he mistakenly pulled me out of my chair, assuming I needed help getting up. A manicurist in a nail salon made me feel subhuman in a million different ways before she forgot to adjust the water temperature for a pedicure and then played havoc with my cuticles. Did she treat everyone the same? Hard to tell. But she never looked me in the eyes. She spent the few minutes before I realized what a hopeless situation it all was, looking at a baby in the lap of the patron adjacent to my chair while she sanded my ankles. That's the tough part. One can never be sure.

I could have drifted along listening to what goes on in the coffee shop. I could have contented myself with waiting and remembering, safe again this summer with the air conditioning almost cancelling the heat wave and hoping the electricity did not vanish in the thunderstorms, if they ever came. I could have pulled the drapes and avoided the brown grass and what few flowers remained; but I didn't. Instead, I decided to listen to my new neighbor's plans; and at first that's all I did. Listen. It was a role I knew inside out.

I watched while Sarah Spicer told the moving men where to put her loveseat and where to stack her boxes; so many books that I thought she would need a yard sale before she moved in. Of course, I listened to Sarah thank me for the champagne I left at her door, and I continued listening to her take on the Duke Lacrosse scandal. She lived up the street from the team's white frame house, opposite the East Campus wall. They made a late night practice of peeing in flower pots on the nearby porches. I guess Sarah liked the way I listened, with my eyes on hers, with few words in between.

Sarah Spicer liked my questions too. She told me about her trips abroad and her plans for the fall. She wasn't a braggart—just sure of herself. She told me I would be a fool not to go with her. She assured me that she was not traveling to Paris! No, she was going to Rome for Thanksgiving. "Why Thanksgiving?" I asked. She didn't answer me, but the look on her face spoke for her. Some women won't admit how lonely they are. Thanksgiving is an American holiday, about to herald routines that no longer work. "Christmas follows soon after. Why not go to London in December?" I said.

She didn't answer that question either. Sarah Spicer is a persuasive woman. But before she unpacked her books, two weeks had passed by, and I had written a check for a ticket to Rome, bought a pair of walking shoes at Bloomingdale's, and ordered a vest on line with eight zippered pockets. "The weather in Rome is unpredictable," Sara quoted her travel agent. She and I were eating cannoli from the Alon Bakery in Virginia Highlands. "I don't know how you get through the week without a car," she moved the greasy white box aside and smiled.

What made me go along with her travel plans? I remembered the hour when things got so bad I could no longer count on movies for distraction, so I began to take Sarah seriously. It was a Wednesday morning, the fifth of

July, before the sun came up. I often got up at 6:00, but this morning was different. I didn't want to get up at all. I didn't want to live in the present or consider the future. My eyes were red from crying and I had rented all the newest releases at the library. I had seen some twice. I lay sideways in my bed—holding the pillow against my breasts— and tried to get back to other summers. Why not enjoy my memories while I still had them? I started with the best one. Naturally the phone rang. It was the Southern Poverty Law Center thanking me for a contribution I forgot I made and telling me of a new hate crime somewhere out West. Morris Dees is my hero, but my mind was so worn out that I could not concentrate long enough on his voice mail to hear the name of the state or the crime. I did remember my check book. My heart was pounding when I took it out of my purse. Soon I was too far away from the memory of that other summer, the best one, and it was no use trying to go back. So I wrote the check to Morris Dees and carefully recorded it. As I addressed the envelope, I realized that I was out of stamps. I made no effort to pick up the envelope from the floor where it had fallen. I was bone tired.

The New York Times became another disappointment. The war. The 2008 election. Scandals and corruption. Even the Arts section had nothing I wanted to read: Hollywood and TV folks constantly rewarding themselves with prizes and now *Sundance* had become so commercial and crowded that it has run away with itself. This week Randy Newman had a poem on the editorial page of the *Atlanta Journal-Constitution* about the decline of the West, and he wasn't talking about the Rocky Mountains! The poem was doggerel, not up to his usual lyric level, and not weird enough for my taste either; but who can argue with his position? He knows right from wrong. He also knows all about floods, oil companies and New Orleans. He grew up there.

Sometimes headlines are all I have stomach for. No sooner did I kiss a long bout with the flu farewell, do I confront death in every headline. More about the War. Then *James Brown* in bold black letters, dead in Crawford Long Hospital, a week before the ball will drop in Times Square with Anderson Cooper at the mike. There were tears in my eyes. Guy Lombardo is long gone, but alive in my memory. I know nothing about James Brown but his loud mouth, stint in prison, and birthplace in South Carolina, but I was drawn to his message assaulting my ears: "I feel good... .I knew that I would." I can't remember the connecting words, just the beginning and end of that refrain. I can't remember the name of the man who held the mike on New Year's Eve in the intervening years – counting, as the ball dropped. I only know that man had a stroke, and it affected his speech. I know, too, that I do not feel so good. All I can think about is me. I am so far from the old days when New Year's Eve meant fancy parties, or supper for two, or just brandy in front of the TV and a few sparklers on the back porch. More than anything, I long for Wes beside me here.

Chapter 25

Things continued to deteriorate. The weather filled my mind and ruined my dreams. Surreal images of fog, rotting row boats moored in the mud of lakes where weeds reached the oars, still attached, but useless. Sleek cars stuck in snow banks with their emergency lights beaming a red staccato into the darkness. "Where is help?" I thought. Not from the weatherman, because future predictions become even more ominous. Yet I walk out into a 70 degree day with the sun already warming my arms. It is January, and though rain may be predicted for the end of the week, in no way does this uneven reality add up to winter.

I try to be realistic. I copy facts in a spiral notebook on the coffee shop counter. Here drought. Here bottled water in every grocery cart. Here facts in my spiral amount to a useless list. But there can be no real preparation because Atlanta drinking water may be gone in four months. Swimming pools may close in the spring. Every TV channel has an expert. How can we live without water? Where can I move? To a state with fires that last for months and destroy everything? To floods that move from the East Coast to the Midwest? To blizzards in Maine where winds take away lamplight, heat, and shelter? Where winds demolish phone lines and make even rich folks with generators worry. I'm sick of the endless predictions on my TV screen and afraid to listen to the dialogue of denial that I know will fill the coffee shop by lunch time. So I order a cup to go and recklessly leave a dollar under my spoon.

Chapter 26

If my reason for getting up in the morning now is to read the obits, it's not hard to roll over and grab a down pillow for the smell and the softness, and then ease myself into a morning dream. The last conversation I overheard at the coffee shop doesn't make me want to return: "Not many people would hire a blind interior decorator. She must have been a family friend." As I walked away, I heard the response, "No, just cut-rate!" I can't figure this joke out. Maybe it wasn't a joke. I can't be sure.

Last summer I bought a vibrator and I use it in the afternoons, weekdays. Frying current makes a steady noise. When I was fourteen, my mother slept with a plumber up the street, and I thought of where his dirty fingernails might go and wept. She cried too—sometimes with the bedroom door closed. So I hung out at the library or read books alone in my room, waiting. I dreamed of escape. I dreamed of money, safety and respect. Now I have money and respect and a vibrator. I think of my mother and wish I had not called her those names. When I flick the switch and try to drift, nothing happens and it takes a long time to come.

Chapter 27

At 6:00 AM everything but the traffic on Shallowford Road seemed to be moving slower than usual: the moon, a full one, was still visible in the daylight; the sun was resting somewhere, but not outside my bedroom window; and my mind, what's left of it, was only letting in what felt good—namely the silky side of my comforter. April 21st…predicted to be sunny and warm, the month drawing to an end. Sinatra in my ears from a dream: "You're riding high in April, shot down in May." Yesterday's tortellini sealed tight in the fridge. *The Times* would have to wait. I went back to sleep.

After my new pattern of only reading headlines and topic sentences, of scanning the obits, I was at last able to concentrate on a two-part article in the morning paper. An Atlanta lawyer with a contagious strain of drug-resistant TB, against medical advice, managed to marry in Paris and return to the U.S. by way of Canada—without being stopped by border guards. His bride's father is a 32-year veteran microbiologist at CDC whose lab investigates the exact strain of TB his son-in-law has now blown through the air of planes and merged with the fragrances of his bride's bouquet at his wedding reception. Did the groom wear a mask on his wedding night? How far does entitlement extend? Does anyone in his confidence feel guilty?

Did the young lawyer work for the government? The powers that be refused to say where he had traveled in the past few years, but he traveled often. These facts made my head spin and unanswered questions whirl inside my brain. What is the common good? Who is protecting whom? When did the bride and her family discover the severity of his condition? Where does denial fit in this picture? And *where does entitlement begin and end?*

My second coffee grew cold, and the lunch trade came and went. I kept on thinking about selfishness, about fear, about this newspaper story and what lies beneath its surface. The story seemed to connect to everything, but then—I kept forgetting parts of it. I can think better in this corner of the coffee shop; but I still can't keep all the connections in place. Am I really slipping? Maybe not. Next to me sits a man who does crosswords every day before he visits his wife who no longer recognizes him. Occasionally he talks to another man about his rose garden. I saw it once—row after row of yellow roses on stakes. A row of corn holds more beauty: the tassels, the green, and the kernels stripped to their golden freshness. Corn belongs in rows—but roses can't flourish strapped to a wooden stake.

Chapter 28

It was not long before I discovered Sarah Spicer Fairbrother is 69. Her husband, a Duke University professor, left her with more than enough money in stocks; so she has rented a three bedroom apartment at the end of the hall. She doesn't need a safety necklace because she owns a Chihuahua named Pucci whose insistent barking gives her the illusion of safety. Its groomer arrives every Friday in a white van and tries to talk her into giving Pucci more than a trim. Sarah has no use for the coffee shop. She, too, plans to swim every morning in the summer and has a hanging device along with a yoga mat already set out in her spare bedroom. She says the device helps her bad back. Sarah thinks nothing of driving to Whole Foods, but she has yet to add theatre to her forays. Instead she talks about Italy steadily and in the end convincingly. Sometimes she shares her take-out with me in the evenings, and every Friday we watch Italian movies on her flat screen TV. Things are going faster than they should, but I can admit at last to loneliness, now that she has made a dent in it. She even got the caretaker to make an exception for Pucci. Maybe she bribed him.

We began our travel preparations with a heavy coffee table book I had checked out of the library. At first Sarah Spicer skipped from one tantalizing Italian city to another, sometimes confusing Venice with Vienna and misquoting Hemingway—stopping only to visit the bathroom. We were sitting on my sofa after shutting the door on the maze of packing boxes still in her bedroom. She met me at every turn with reassurance, "Cruises are made for old people," she was positive. "You'll relax into it. A library, deck chairs, two pools. Even room service is free. You can stay in your room and stare at the waves if the crowds are too much for you." I let her talk.

Sarah Spicer wore me down. It took a week of her steady, soft southern voice. I listened. Yes. But I also resisted with a series of *what ifs*? What if the cathedral steps were too steep, the cobblestones slick, the air conditioning unreliable? How can medical care abroad be safe? The doctors speak Italian, don't they? What about lines at the airport: masses of people taking their shoes off and shoving them in plastic tubs, bells ringing, wheelchairs everywhere reminding us of what the future has in store? Sarah Spicer acknowledged Europe wasn't air conditioned, and at first she tried to answer me, point by point; but she soon just pushed on with her own examples and an occasional smile. She finally enticed me with images of a whirlwind trip through Italy on a bus to see real landscapes, not coffee table art! All that stunning religious imagery, the David, a million Madonnas... . She painted our days wide with possibilities. "All right," I said finally. "But only if you make all the arrangements."

"Don't forget I speak Italian," Sarah countered as she shut her apartment door. It was as though all that possibility finally broke into my rituals and left me with hope, but also with things I never wanted to remember. Yes, I drifted through that whole afternoon recapturing: an August day 40 years ago, heat, and a fair haired boy from Choate pinning my hands to a dirty gray carpet while I pleaded, begged and screamed; as he, wordless, entered and pounded until he was finished with me. He lost no time in leaving my ragged apartment; and though we had planned two library dates that week, I never saw him again. I thought I would. Any day. Someday. I couldn't imagine the possible variations of rape in those years. And I blamed myself. That fall, I never used my season tickets to the Hartford Stage because I wasn't sure if it was his blue blazer just ahead of me opening night in line at the box office. In my dreams, sometimes he wears a seersucker suit. Sometimes his old topsiders are covered with mud. Always, some part of his preppie uniform is ruined. Tweeds outgrown, cardigans unraveled, his telltale gray jockey shorts clutter these dreams. But I am the one soiled. For me, a nap is never just a nap. Often it is a horror show. And what does it all have to do with a predictable week in Italy with card-carrying AARP members? I wish I knew.

Friday night became Saturday morning. I lost track of my nightmare and the time once I found my remote in the bed clothes and pressed "CH". Pulled right into *The Today Show* with the words, "funny man," and a shot of George Carlin on an empty stage, I first thought he must have a new HBO special but then I heard the past tense push his life off the screen. I tried hard to be optimistic about our Italian trip. I got out of bed and stood in front of my window and made a list of outfits to pack in my suitcase.

I had wanted to forget last Saturday night when, for the first time since I moved here, I accepted an invitation to a party here in the complex. Sarah had planned to go too, but she chickened out at the last minute. A birthday celebration. Air conditioning on high instead of the night air. One frail woman even wore a cotton sweater. Everyone was older than I. At least they appeared to be. One woman leaned on lilac flowers twirled with sparkles set deep in a Lucite cane. More than one black cane rested in an umbrella stand beside a walker. Footstools were at a premium. I was lucky to find a wing chair only two steps from the door.

Why did I go? Curiosity? Proximity? Loneliness? This segregated evening stretched on and on and required few words from me. *Maybe I wanted to kill time.*

"May I share your footstool?" a man declared. He was on a sofa jammed up against my chair. "Do you keep busy?" He reminded me of that condescending OB GYN nurse I have tried to forget.

"Well, I like to look out the window. This year I've been busy remembering my husband. He jumps out at me in dreams too." The man didn't know what to say.

"They have Sangria," he pointed to a pitcher on a table shoved up against the wall.

"I hate red wine. It stains."

Just then the birthday girl walked by eating some spinach and dough confection we used to order in Greek restaurants when my husband was alive. In fact, when the lines were long and we didn't have reservations, the owner offered samples to make the wait easier to bear. I took one and hoped they were drinking more than Sangria tonight. At that point, the man fished two of those tiny bottles they serve on airplanes out of his pocket and offered one to me. It was Jack Daniels, and it wasn't cold.

"Jack Black is good all year round," he grinned. Does this mean he's an alcoholic? Or, perhaps, an aging boy scout?

"Do you have a napkin tucked away as well?" He shook his head. Just then, what appeared to be a teenager asked if he could get me something.

"A glass of ice," I smiled, "I need to cool off."

"I'll have one too," said the man. Somewhere between trying to pour the whiskey and not attract attention and introducing ourselves, I relaxed. This wasn't so different from a real cocktail party. Everyone was sitting down, some a little more bent than others. Across the room I saw a woman with an asthma blower. You might even call it an old fashioned evening. Men talked. Women listened. Men bragged; but it was my *successful* children, my *devoted* grandchildren. Nobody mentioned gas prices. Here and there I could hear phrases that indicated the stock market was plunging again, and early retirement had been a *big* mistake.

The whiskey was no better or worse than it had ever been. "Have you ever visited that town in Tennessee where they make it?" The man's voice had a slight tremor.

"Make what?" I succumbed to small talk.

"Jack Daniels," he replied.

"I don't need to. The package store kept me supplied when my husband was alive, and now I buy wine next door at Publix. I don't drive any more. You remember the store on LaVista and Oak Grove, the one where a customer came in and blew the owner's brains out? It's a dry cleaners now."

"Yes, they do leather and wedding dresses," I had hoped we might go a little deeper into this thin air, yet there seemed little chance of it now.

"When did you have your first drink?" For some reason, I dredged up a story for him—one I'd told a hundred times with much more animation.

"When? I was in college and everyone else drank beer. One night at a party my roommate and I were served warm vodka in a jelly glass. Must have been two shots each. One drink on an empty stomach and we decided to walk back to the dorm! I threw up on the sidewalk. She grabbed a light pole and twirled around it saying, 'The room is spinning!' The party had been in a Victorian house owned by a professor who rented rooms to grad students. We had been packed in a front bedroom with a song, *Was there ever such a night? You could see the midnight sun.* I can't remember what I ate yesterday, but I remember song lyrics from that party, not their titles. All I know for sure is that mention was made of the Aurora Borealis."

"Never heard it. My first drink came from my father's liquor cabinet. Straight from the bottle. No evidence leftover."

I managed to leave this man eventually, remarkably steady on my feet. Out the door—without thanking the hostess, sorry I'd come in the first place. Later, alone here in my bedroom, I bring back my memory of a first glimpse of Italy with roots going all the way back to 1964 when I was working mornings doing free lance editing. I kept the manuscripts on my night stand, along with sharpened pencils and red pens. The requisite brown envelopes lay in a kitchen drawer already stamped. We had an AM/FM radio. I saved the music for the late afternoons and we listened to the news before supper if Wes wasn't on call. The cities were burning that summer: Newark, Detroit... I'm not sure about Chicago...why can't I remember the others? Newark's brown air and ugliness was unmatched by any city I'd yet seen; but I was safe in Hartford inside our air conditioned apartment and after a dish of ice cream for lunch, I brought out a library copy of *The Italians* by Luigi Barzini and dreamed about a future when Wes and I could spend a whole month there. Later, I bought my own copy. I still have it. Underlined with pages unglued, some fallen away. Forty years later.

That summer, I read a chapter or two of Barzini each day along with a novel. I think it was *Madame Bovary*. I didn't want either book to end, and I didn't want to confront the heat. I wanted the unending dream that some critic says a work of fiction should be. I took out coffee table books from the library then too and stared at the ruins of the Roman Coliseum as I thought about the barbarism that once played itself out as a stylized game, different from the fires that burned in Newark and Harlem; at night I dreamed about Madame Bovary and her safe, stolid husband—the boring doctor. Those early years at the Institute, doctors worried and talked about what could and couldn't be done while I once heard a patient singing through the screen in an open window, "What have they done to my brain, Ma?" Or was it, Mom? The song filled the radio stations that August and then subsided with the heat. By the time I actually went to Italy with Sarah, I needed a new, larger copy of *The Italians* with big print. It would have been so much easier to just stay home in bed, I thought on the plane. But I pushed these regrets out of my mind.

I first saw the Roman Coliseum at night (Sarah Spicer had jet lag) on a bus from the hotel making its last ride there and back. I was the only passenger. It had rained that day and now we were left with a mist. The driver eventually stopped and walked inside a bar across the cobblestone street from where the bus was parked. Three cats chased each other out the door. There was not another person in sight. The driver returned after a bit with a lit cigarette in his mouth. The moonlit ruins would have to wait until morning. The ride back to the hotel didn't take long. The hotel lobby was empty, but a crowd of Japanese businessmen stood at the cappuccino bar. I took the elevator up. Sarah Spicer was asleep. I stubbed my toe, but she didn't move.

The rest of the trip was easy. How difficult is sitting on a high, cushiony seat on a bus with all of the restaurants selected ahead of time with clean hotels and spas attached? And young clerks who speak English and could have popped out of a forties film—in starched white collars and navy blue suits. The tour guides were professors and librarians, not bored housewives who had memorized a pamphlet. Questions from the passengers were thoughtful. Nary a showboat among them. A few depressed widows arrived alone, but they got acquainted with each other by the end of the week; and the unmarried tour guide, who lived in Scotland most of the year, was especially kind to them. Sarah Spicer talked on and on to anyone who would listen about how much she missed the Duke campus. She brought out some little cigars which attracted the attention of an old man who joined the group in Florence and trailed after the tour guide—giving the impression that he was in training for her job until Sarah caught his eye. They spent a lot of time together when the bus stopped smoking those little cigars.

Chapter 29

After we flew home, Sarah methodically wrote letters to the two widows. I didn't see her for two weeks.

I am alone now. More and more, the rooms I have here seem like a treasure, and I don't want to leave them. It's been months since the last power outage, so the stove and the lights, the computer and the radio (my TV has lost its sound) bring me what matters. Why should I go out this door? Oh, some mornings I miss the coffee shop; but Bachner takes more and longer trips now, so I can't count on his politics or his chivalry or his loud voice which, in itself, is a comfort. Unlike a radio dial, I can't adjust the sounds real people make. Last week I dropped my coffee cup there, and the crockery chips scattered on the floor and scared a little boy who started crying. The owner promised to stencil my name on a new one, and in the meantime I drink out of the standard paper cups. Their lids are tight. They feel safe. I haven't dropped one yet, but it's not the same. I feel I've lost something more than yellow pottery.

I can't dwell on loss. There is too much of it. I try to think about what's left and what matters; and my mind wanders back to parks I've loved. After all, it's April again and whoever said it is the cruelest month was wrong. In Atlanta, even from my window, I know how long the dogwood blooms and how the wisteria hangs off the trees near my door. Memories matter. Whether it's those postage stamp parks wedged between skyscrapers in Manhattan, the azaleas and the marble fountain in back of Callanwolde, or the expansive grounds at The Institute of Living in Hartford, I can close my eyes and bring them all back. Safe here in my recliner, once in a while, I even dream about how it felt to know I could sit on benches, wooden or stone, and sink into the spell they create. You could say, off and on, I can bring all of that greenery inside my bedroom. Sometimes, I even smell the cut grass when I wake up from a nap.

Bachner bought me a pristine copy of *A Ticket to the Circus*, a memoir by Norris Church. Being married to Norman Mailer for 30 years and loving him, in spite of it all, seems like an old fashioned accomplishment. I felt sad when I finished the final page; all the literary gossip, personal honesty and escapades! She took over the scutwork, balanced his accounts in that apartment in Brooklyn overlooking the water, and gradually set it straight. She had what I never had, real confidence, not bravado. She was stepmother to his seven and had two of her own. It made me cry when they gathered at her bedside, more than once, and stayed around the clock through her bouts with cancer. I have regrets, and missing out on children is one of them; so I envy Norris Church at their Provincetown house all those summers and holidays—happy. I don't like endings, and she is a physical wreck inside now—still a beauty though—in her high-necked, vivid cover up! But her days are numbered. Mine are too.

Chapter 30

A month passed. Just when I was feeling too tired to boil an egg, who shows up but Bachner. Of course, he called first to find out if I was in the middle of a television show or a TV dinner. It was his way of being polite. I'd told him that my sound is gone. So within the hour, he arrived with a loaf of brown bread from Whole Foods, still warm, and turtle soup. I didn't ask where he got it, but it didn't come from a can. I smiled and brought out a bottle of cream sherry to add a little spark to the occasion and poured some in the soup before I filled two tiny glasses.

Bachner never talks about his real social life, but the coffee shop is just his jumping off point, I am sure. Bachelors are always in demand: the extra man at a dinner party; one of the three male students in a photography class. He also volunteers at a hospice facility. Imagine all those other widows. He and I lingered so long that I had to reheat the soup.

"The last time I had turtle soup," I told him, "Wes and I were in the courtyard of Commander's Palace in New Orleans surrounded by a jazz trio filling the air with old Louis Armstrong favorites."

"They really keep that paint fresh on the outside," was all he said.

Bachner thinks like the landlord that he is. I took my time putting away the leftovers after he was gone. National Public Radio was interviewing a man who wrote a book about modern parents and their estranged children. At least I don't have that kind of loss to contend with. Then I went to bed to enjoy a long spell with Garrison Keillor. His intro has grown on me, but the first time I heard him sign off from Lake Wobegon where "all the women are strong, all the men are good looking, and all the children are above average," I thought he was a sap. Now his voice on Saturday night is a pleasure I count on, and the ad for biscuits cracks me up; though I can't remember the brand. Maybe I am losing my memory. I hope not. If I fall asleep before the end of the show, I needn't worry because NPR repeats it on Sunday morning at ten.

Chapter 31

Some animal stories on TV are beyond me. A woman trained a chimp to drink wine, eat meals in a chair, bathe and sleep with her. And that was just the beginning. There must have been more in the middle, but the ending was sudden. It was a matter of nerves. The chimp was nervous, so the woman shared her medicine with it; but something didn't fit and the chimp tore off her friend's face. All those years of successful behavior modification went out the window when help came with a bullet. 911 sent the police, not a doctor!

I remember reading about a loyal dog in New York City, a protective German Shepherd. His owner was a young mother who had lost her job and was trying to get on welfare. She waited and nursed her baby. She and the dog grew thinner. Their bones showed through their skin, in places. One day, she left the baby at home with the animal while she walked to the Society of Saint Vincent de Paul for a crib and a high chair. She waited in line for food stamps first, but her application forms had not "gone through." Encouraged by the kindness of the social worker, she rolled the crib home on its little casters and through the door of her ground level apartment. Only the dog was waiting for her.

Nobody from Nebraska came to the city for the funeral. Those two women had high expectations—at least in the beginning. Now who can tell what comes next? Their real story remains untold. Their animals only starred in the introductions. Tonight the rain beats on the windows, and I can see a roach huddled in the corner where the wooden floors meet the brown bathroom tiles.

Chapter 32

Lately, now that the pool is closed and drained for the season, even though the trees hang onto their leaves and an occasional afternoon is sunny and warm, I do little more than brush my teeth in the morning and stare out the window. Black outside, with traffic stopping and starting and the street lamps around the pool still lit. I look in the mirror and wonder how it has all come to this: bags under my eyes that never look darker because I've used Erase for the last 20 years, yet now they bulge every so slightly. On such mornings, a shower is easy to avoid. I don't want to face up to a body with more sag than my face will ever show. Instead I open the front door, bend to retrieve the blue plastic bag and carry it back to my bed. I keep bottled water on my bedside table, so I use it to take the vitamins I laid out the night before. Then I slide back under my quilt. Some days I fall asleep. Most times, I draw unruly circles around the headlines that worry me most, read the editorials I know I'll agree with, and then methodically move backwards to the front page. Things have settled down in New Orleans though President Bush comes and goes for photo-ops. This morning he arrived with Laura at his side. Maureen Dowd can be counted on to flatten him and move on to his cronies. Did she say Cheney's new office is in the back of an ambulance? Or was it Gail Collins? It's easy to be a smart ass—even easier to throw darts when you are part of a pack. "Always kick a man when he's down; you'll never get a better chance". I'm ashamed to admit my uncle, as he grew older and lost what was left of his mind, could be counted on to repeat this piece of vitriol at every family party we ever had!

Bachner is about to visit his sister in Jersey. He is wearing an orange sticker to let everyone know he voted. "I'll drive you to the polls when I get back; then we'll both be ahead of the game." I don't ask where he's going in the interim. I don't ask if his sister is sick or when he's coming back to Atlanta. He is a man of his word. Like Wes. Like Dr. Lawler. "Let yourself out" I say, knowing he has a key. Knowing how delicious my nap is going to be, almost forgetting Halloween. "Trick or treat" is the slogan at the coffee shop, and the owner is baking mini cupcakes for the children. In the North, we called out "Help the poor," as the bravest of us knocked on the screen doors. We called it "begging" and all of us managed to come up with a torn pillow case to hold our loot and a costume. We were limited, though: bums, witches or angels. We left our porches covered by cast off play clothes, tattered funeral dresses, and the whitest of bleached sheets—confident in these disguises that cost nothing—feeling on top of the world! We returned after dark with pennies, rotten apples, every variety of one cent candy the A & P carried, and the remote possibility of a candy bar. Rumor had it that the drunk at the end of the street once handed out quarters; but the oldest among us knew it was a lie.

Deadpan humor is hard to sort out from ordinary facts, and somewhere before I open the Arts Section of the New York *Times*, the excitement that I've felt for years passes away. On such mornings, I would leave disheveled, if I didn't pull out the simplest of costumes—corduroy pants, a pair of clogs lined in fur, and a turtleneck—all gray. Of course I wear underwear because I like the feel of it. Almost like a transitional object that replaces the proverbial "blankie" in Snoopy cartoons. On such mornings, the coffee shop matters most. My mood is black. A random misery. I never know when to expect it. I'm tempted to take a seat in the back where businessmen set up shop with their requisite cell phones and laptops. I long to hide there and listen to the music. Before the morning crowd leaves, something will happen though; something will be said that changes things for me. It can be as slight a change as peach muffins replacing the Russian tea biscuits or Bachner looking grim and needing me to cheer him up. Today it was a teenage girl who smiled at me. Not completely overlooked, I think.

Talk centers on winters up North, and, as usual, Bachner takes the lead. "What we need here is an electric fireplace; the kind with heat and flames but no mess." I let him talk. The sun coming in the windows is enough for me today. But I listen to him tell about cutting down trees, green logs, splitting wood, fall in Jersey; and I only tune out when sleep threatens to overtake me. Bachner takes note of a blonde at the head of the coffee line. She wears a vest of rabbit fur over a black jump suit. I raise my eyebrows. She's tired, like the rest of us, but unfailingly polite. I have seen her here before. Always early and always alone. The vest makes her look protected. By the time she takes her cup to a table, I can see she's sitting across from a woman with a suitcase on wheels and a matching cosmetic case in the third chair. "If anything happens to me on my flight, I want you to have my husband because he would be good to you!" I don't want to hear the rest of this conversation, but I don't want to leave either; so I ask Bachner about what to expect on T.V. All he tells me is that Mike Logan (Chris Noth) is coming back to *Law and Order* after ten years away as Mr. Big in *Sex and the City*. It's *Law and Order: Criminal Intent*, Bachner makes sure I know the program begins on Sunday night. Such suggestions are like gifts; and I live on them. Everything seems so much more than it appears to be now that I am on the other side of 80.

Chapter 33

The new clerk was nervous. She had listened carefully as the owner showed her a pile of tee shirts with the coffee shop logo and a whole row of prepackaged coffee. Baristas come and go. College only lasts so long even if you work your way through. Eventually new help must be found. Training takes time, patience. Stenciled coffee cups for the regulars sit next to the French Roast on the shelf above the paper cups. There is a lot to remember. Moving fast and still holding onto your smile in a morning rush doesn't come easy. It's a serious business. Other applicants are waiting in the wings if you can't pull it off. The owner keeps those resumes in three bulging file folders!

"Whose coffee is it?" the barista said for the second time. The bathroom door was locked and the two customers at the counter did not look up. The barista continued filling a large phone order of Lattés while a teenager tapped her espadrilles on the chair leg and watched the milk in her Venti gradually lighten and swirl. She had decided to skip school.

The old woman on the sofa was asleep.

"Did someone just leave this coffee here?" the barista's voice was well modulated and her words were distinct.

It seemed like a stupid thing to say; but even if it was, nobody answered. So the barista went on filling sugar containers because she had been warned to keep working although the rush had subsided. She wiped off the counter and thought how clean this place was. She had worked in coffee shops before, and she knew that not all stainless steel kept its shine. The lull continued until a tall man with white hair walked through the door. He thought the old woman was asleep too, at first. After all, how many women her age leave this world, alone, with customers all around them, without a gasp or a slump? Her head rested against the window pane, and the *New York Times* lay folded in her lap.

Biography

Recipient of a 2001 Yaddo Writers' Fellowship, June Akers Seese is also the author of two novels published by Dalkey Archive Press: *What Waiting Really Means, Is This What Other Women Feel Too?*, plus a collection of short fiction, *James Mason and the Walk-In Closet. Some Things are Better Left to Saxophones* and *A Nurse Can Go Anywhere and Collected Short Stories* were published by iUniverse.

Her short stories have appeared in *Witness, Carolina Quarterly,* and *South Carolina Review,* and they are collected in three chapbooks funded by the Georgia Council for the Arts: *Near Occasions of Sin, Claudia and a Long Line of Women,* and *My Affairs are in Order/All Those Men are Dead Now.*.

Mrs. Seese teaches "The Memoir: Reading It and Writing It" at Callanwolde Fine Arts Center in Atlanta, Georgia.